Chain Reaction

Also by Lee Jordan

The Toy Cupboard
The Deadly Side of the Square

Chain Reaction

Lee Jordan

Walker and Company
New York

Copyright © 1989 by Lee Jordan

All rights reserved. No part of this book may be reproduced or transmitted in any form or by any means, electronic or mechanical, including photocopying, recording, or by any information storage and retrieval system, without permission in writing from the Publisher.

All the characters and events portrayed in this work are fictitious.

First published in the United States of America in 1993
by Walker Publishing Company, Inc.

Originally published in Great Britain.

Library of Congress Cataloging-in-Publication Data
Lee Jordan
Chain reaction / Lee Jordan.
    p.   cm.
ISBN 0-8027-1249-5
1. Women detectives—France—Fiction. I. Title.
PR6060.06254C48   1993
823'.914—dc20   93-16458
                      CIP

Printed in the United States of America

2 4 6 8 10 9 7 5 3 1

0

The man no longer looked like a man. There was blood on his head and face, and a growth on his back.

In the dust-filled darkness he lay on his stomach and dragged himself over the rubble on his elbows, giving the impression of some great reptile.

On he came.

Each time he pushed an elbow into the ground and heaved, his body twisted in the way a saurian moves across dry land.

It was ungainly and exhausting.

But even though he was dying, this man, whom people had often likened to a forest troll, still had power in his thick, short arms.

On he came.

Elbow after elbow.

In the small area that survived of his mind, like the corner of a dimly lit room, he knew what he had to do.

Ahead he could see a face; a white amorphous shape like a small moon.

That's what spurred him on. The need to smash it. Obliterate it.

On he came.

Painfully slowly. A misshapen, legless alligator.

1

Alex Bridgman picked up the phone and dialled David's private line. She could see his office in her mind's eye. The windows looked out on to London's Curzon Street. The room itself was small but the desk was of English yew with a green leather top. The rest of the room was shelves of books and piles of manuscripts.

The phone rang twice and then she heard his voice.
'David Clarke.'
'Hello, David Clarke.'
'Hi. This is nice.'
She could see him leaning back in his chair, a smile on his face – at least she hoped he was smiling.
'Are you smiling?'
'Why?'
'Just curious. Listen . . . Oh, by the way, can you talk?'
'I'm alone.'
'I had a lunch date with Robin Akers of *The Chronicle*'s magazine section. But he's had to cancel.'
She waited.
'And?' he said.
'Well, you know, I thought . . .'
'Is this a proposition?'
'What do you think?'
'Damn, I've got a lunch.' She could hear him flick

over his diary pages. 'Twelve-thirty. With Dick Timmins at the Savile.'

'Put him off. It's not as though he's an important author.'

He laughed. 'Authors aren't the only import—'

'He's another publisher. All you'll do is sit around and tell each other lies about the big advances you've paid to so and so, or the – quote – distinguished books you're doing for Christmas. Or would you rather not?'

'Of course I'd not rather not. I'll put him off. But there may be a problem with the flat at this short notice. I'll call you back.'

Alex stood for a moment at the long windows of her flat in Swiss Cottage, then went and had a shower. She stood under the spray and turned up the heat as high as she could stand, then cut it and let the water run cold. She towelled herself and fossicked through her drawers for underclothing. Everything looked as if it had come from Oxfam.

She wished the flat was nearer the West End, then he could come to her.

As she dressed she looked at herself in the long mirror by the window. She saw a tall woman, leggy and long-striding, with high breasts and a fair, almost Nordic complexion. She twisted her upper body one way, then the next. She had never liked her shoulders. Too square.

Her tennis coach – in the days when she was one of the country's junior hopes – had said they were what she needed for a big serve. But all that had come to an end one day at Queens when she had been on court for nearly three hours in a junior grass courts final, and had suddenly thought: 'You can't go on playing games all your life!'

So she'd gone to university instead and taken a degree

in modern languages, learned photography in her spare time, then presented herself, all shiny new and keen as mustard, to several editors in Fleet Street.

Degree? Photography? They had spoken the words as though they might catch something nasty. What about experience?

She'd moved to the provinces for a couple of years and had then found a job in London on one of the weekend colour magazines that were proliferating at the time.

She'd stayed five years, gained experience and made a lot of contacts. She could get a story and write it and bring it in on time. She was professional. Now, at twenty-seven, she was a freelance and beginning to make a name for herself.

She pulled out a pair of tights. They were laddered. Why stuff them back in the drawer then? she asked herself angrily.

Sometimes she thought she was a slut. Her mother would have agreed. But everyone's mothers thought that about their daughters, didn't they?

The phone rang. She paused. Fingers crossed.

David said, 'All set. When?'

She felt her heart pick up a beat. 'I'll be outside the office at twelve.'

'Make it quarter past.'

'See you.'

At mid-morning of that same day the little village of Carriac on the Dordogne River in France was counting its dead. By the time Alex had found a taxi on the Finchley Road, the total number of bodies stood at fifteen.

Ten hours earlier Carriac had been one of the dream villages of the Dordogne. It lay on the middle river, between Beynac and Souillac, and the nearest town of any importance was Sarlat.

It had grown over the centuries between the great green river and the limestone cliffs that give this part of the Dordogne much of its beauty.

The cliffs rose more than a hundred feet above the valley and allowed just enough space for a ribbon-like village to be built along its base. Between the village houses and the river itself there was room only for a narrow road.

At times of heavy rain the river flooded the road and the first row of houses. Once it had even reached the second row. But never the third. The village was three rows wide, each row being six or eight feet higher than the one in front. The last row was built against the cliff-face itself.

All that summer the rain had never been far off and the river had run high. Spring had been wet and so too had the previous winter.

Many of the locals could not remember a wetter period. They shook their heads in gloom. The number of tourists – the life-blood of the village – was down by almost twenty per cent.

One storm had followed another, its lightning crackling overhead.

The previous night had been hot and sultry, and towards midnight, without any warning, a section of the cliff above the village had collapsed.

One moment, in a dozen houses in the centre of Carriac, people had been watching TV, having baths, reading in bed, sleeping. The next, the houses were flattened under thousands of tons of rock and many of the inhabitants were dead.

Ten hours later some order had been brought to the chaos. The *sapeurs-pompiers* had come from Sarlat and

Souillac, bulldozers had been brought in and a mobile crane had arrived from Brive. Ambulances had taken the dead and injured to hospital and a line still waited for more.

And there were more. As the great rocks were lifted from what had once been sitting-rooms and bathrooms and kitchens, in which the cookers and fridges had been squashed flat, it became apparent that there were still other bodies under the rubble.

One of them was a young Englishman named Neville Johnson. He was nineteen years old and part of a foreign community that had long lived in Carriac.

His mother, Mary, had been with him for hours, holding his hand and encouraging him while the rescuers tried to raise the heavy oak beams which lay across him.

He had been one of the first to go to the rescue of others and had been trapped himself when a wall collapsed.

He was a hero.

2

Alex sat in the taxi near the publishing house of Byrom & Lancing and watched for David. She had told the driver to park in a side street some distance from the entrance. Several familiar faces came out of the building and strolled in the direction of the Shepherd's Market restaurants. Then she saw him. He was hard to miss: tall, fast-moving, longish dark hair blowing in the slight breeze and a face, someone had once said, that looked like an American Indian.

He stopped at the taxi, gave the driver the address in Bayswater, and flung himself on to the seat.

'Hi,' he said.

'Hi yourself.'

As the taxi drove off he pulled her towards him and kissed her.

When their lips finally came unglued, she drew breath and said, 'Wow!'

'Wow indeed.' He glanced at the taxi driver. 'I wish he'd hurry up!'

But the traffic was heavy and it took nearly five minutes to get on to Park Lane.

'How long have we got?' she said.

'I've got to be back at two-fifteen. Murdoch's coming in.'

'The Dirty Digger?'

'No. Andrew Murdoch. He wants to talk about his new book.'

'It's not very long.'

'It's the best I could do.'

'Darling, I'm not complaining.'

'If we were married none of this need happen.'

She did not reply and the silence hung between them like a barrier. He leaned back and lit a cigarette. Instantly the cabbie slid the partition window open and said, 'No smoking. Can't you see the sign?'

David took one more draw and put the cigarette out. Alex saw his face contract in irritation and said hastily, 'I bought some gravadlax and brown bread and a couple of bottles of Riesling.'

'Dill sauce?'

'Of course.'

'You're fantastic.'

'I know.'

He began to nibble the lobe of her ear. 'Not many people know about ear-lobes. Why do you think God gave them to us?'

'To hang earrings on?'

'Have another guess.'

The flat, a pied-à-terre which belonged to a wealthy friend of David's, was in one of the new blocks just off the Edgware Road in what was being called the 'Arab Quarter.' They reached it at twelve-thirty.

David opened the door, closed it, and they stood in the little dark hall, wound round each other like ivy. Then she froze. 'David!' she whispered.

'What?'

'There's someone in the flat!'

The loudest thing in the hall was their breathing as they strained to hear. There was a clinking sound from down the hall. Alex moved softly towards it in stockinged feet.

The flat comprised a sitting/dining-room, a bedroom, a bathroom and a small kitchen. She knew the layout well.

The sounds were coming from the bathroom. She stopped near the door and craned to see. David was behind her.

A pair of dirty trainers were sticking out into the bathroom doorway. They were at the bottom of a pair of legs which seemed to disappear under the loo.

She edged forward and looked round the doorframe. A man was working at the base of the cistern, his head on the far side of the pan.

'It's a plumber,' she hissed.

'What the hell's he doing here?'

'Fixing something, I suppose.'

They retreated to the bedroom, which contained a large double-bed and a row of built-in cupboards and not much else. He closed the door. 'Wouldn't you know it!'

'Sssh!'

They sat on the bed, where they had so often sported with each other. She took his hand and held it to her cheek. 'Never mind, he'll go soon.'

'Maybe if I helped . . . '

'You . . . ' She fought a fit of laughter.

He laughed silently with her. 'You think I can't fix things?'

He went back into the passage, opened the front door and closed it with a bang. Then went down the passage to the bathroom.

The plumber was sitting up. He was a youngish man with the bulging muscles of a body-builder.

'Hi,' David said. 'Something wrong?'

The plumber gave him the look of a man who is asked this question fifty times a day. 'Leak,' he said. 'Going down to the flat underneath.'

'You nearly done?'

'Why? You want to use the bathroom?'

'Well, no, not just at the minute. My secretary and I have come here to get some peace so we can work.'

The plumber looked at him straight-faced. 'You get on with it, mate. I won't interfere.'

'Is there anything I can do?'

'In what way?'

'Well . . . hand you things . . . ?'

The plumber did not reply.

David went back to the bedroom. 'Independent. Doesn't want any help.'

'Look, why don't we have our food and by that time he might have gone.'

They went into the kitchen and ate the gravadlax and drank some wine.

They waited. The minutes ticked by.

'This is hopeless!' David said.

She kissed him, tasting the salmon on his lips. 'He'll be gone in a minute.'

'Maybe he's replumbing the entire flat! Listen, I've got an idea. What about tonight? I could come round to your – Oh blast! No, I couldn't. Simon's in a school play. I have to go.' Simon was David's nine-year-old son. 'Why don't you come, too, and then afterwards . . . '

She shook her head. 'That's what mums do, not girlfriends.'

'Simon would love it.' He saw her expression change. 'But you're not his mother, are you.'

'David, I'm sorry, I didn't mean—'

'I know. I know.' He held her close. 'The invitation still stands. The other one.'

'You mean move in?'

'I want you either as my wife or girlfriend or mistress or call it what you like. I just want you. And this isn't the way to do it.'

'What isn't?'

'Being lunchtime lovers. I've looked at my watch twice a minute since we came.'

'Yes. I know. So have I. It'll be better when we go on holiday.'

The plumber came back. 'It's fixed,' he said. 'Cheers.'

It was one-forty-nine when he finally closed the door.

They looked at each other. Each knew what the other was thinking. They cleaned up the kitchen, straightened the bed and then, their arms round each other's waists, walked slowly down the corridor to the elevator.

By late that afternoon the rescue services in Carriac were sure that all the dead and injured had been removed.

The Red Cross had taken some of the homeless to hotels in the area. The village was stunned. At dusk the people gathered at the riverbank and had an impromptu service. Most were in tears.

One man still dug in the rubble for his wife, carrying the stones down to the water and throwing them in. He had been doing so all day long.

He had been told several times that she was dead and had been removed to the mortuary in Sarlat, but he did not believe them. He went on, his hands bleeding, his face and clothing covered in dust, until it grew too dark to see. Only then did he allow himself to be led away by a Red Cross worker.

3

It was a Saturday morning a fortnight later. Alex had been away for two days on a story and had got back late the night before. She planned a lazy day: bath, wash hair, cheese and tomato on toast, a long laze with a book. That was fine for Saturday, but what about Sunday? She lay in the bath brooding about it and was still brooding when she had finished her breakfast and was drying her hair in the summer sunshine on her balcony.

Sunday was a brute. She looked at the phone. David? Sunday was his day with Simon. They went somewhere together. She'd accompanied them several times but had always felt left out.

She wondered what his dead wife, Susan, had really been like. He hardly ever mentioned her.

Since the abortive visit to the flat they had been wary of each other. Maybe they had said too much, maybe too little. That was the problem, she never knew quite how to respond. He talked of marriage, but did he really mean that *he* needed her, or was she wanted to fill the gap left by Susan; in other words, as a mother for Simon?

And she wasn't blaming only him. There was her own ... nervousness. That was the only word for it. She was nervous of the very thought of taking Susan's place. And she was nervous of Simon himself. She could sense his antipathy. She knew he was resenting her. Yet what could she do? If she wanted to go on seeing David she would have to put up with it. Why, oh why, couldn't he have been free, alone, uncomplicated? She'd have married him like a shot.

They were due to leave in a few weeks for Brittany. They would both have preferred ambling slowly through Burgundy, eating and drinking and making love, but that would not have been fair on Simon.

Now that the holiday was nearly upon them she was beginning to feel slightly apprehensive of being so much in Simon's company. What if his resentment turned to something more positive – like hatred?

He was an aloof boy. Old for his years. She couldn't ever recall him giving the slightest indication that he liked her, not even when she brought him presents and went out of her way to be nice to him. But she told herself that his feelings were natural. She would feel the same in his place, having lost a mother and seeing his father with someone else.

The sun went behind a cloud and the street outside became grey and empty. The day loomed ahead of her. David worked on Saturday mornings and she was tempted to phone, suggest he came round to her in the afternoon. But she could almost hear his replies in her head: 'I'm helping Simon fix his bike.' 'Simon's friend is coming round,' 'I'm taking Simon to the Science Museum . . . the movies . . . the theatre . . . the coast . . . '

The phone rang.

Her heart lifted. She grabbed it. 'David?' she said.

'I'm afraid not. It's Robin Akers of *The Chronicle Magazine.*'

'Oh, sorry, I was expecting someone else.'

'Maybe I can make up for it. I tried to get you all yesterday and the day before.'

'I was in Devon.'

'Listen, I've an idea that may interest you. I'm not too far from your place. How about a bite in Hampstead?'

'Lunch?'

'I know it's the weekend, but it could be a good story.'

'Fine.'

'I'll pick you up at twelve-thirty.'

She put down the phone. Well, that was something. Not quite what she would have liked... but something.

Carriac slowly came to terms with the tragedy. The central section had been demolished, cutting the village in two. Part of the rubble had been cleared from the road and people were able to pick their way along a narrow path at the river's edge as they moved to and fro between the *boulangerie* and post office at one end and a small group of shops at the other. The path was controlled by a *gendarme* who kept in touch with the top of the cliffs by walkie-talkie.

Already there were two cranes at the top as well as a dozen or more drilling machines. The strengthening of the cliffs had been started and as the loose and unsafe rock was cut and blasted away the path would be closed and the area evacuated.

The idea was to give the top of the cliff steel and concrete inlays which would hold it together and put an end to rockfalls.

When blasting was to take place an old air raid siren was set off and people hurried out of harm's way. All except the man who still dug for his wife's remains.

He was a Dutchman, Thomas van der Meulen, and he was impervious to sirens or warnings, even to the dynamite explosions which started further, smaller rockfalls. He had to be led away each time. And, when the dust cleared and the chips of stone stopped zinging down into the water and giving the impression of rising fish, he would return to his task of uncovering what remained of his house.

Simon's face was only a matter of inches from the snake. They regarded each other in solemn silence; the pale, serious-faced boy and the long black snake, twined round the branch of a tree. The snake's tongue flickered ceaselessly as it absorbed the vibrations coming from the other side of its glass cage.

David and Alex stood some way back, allowing Simon to be swept along with the crowd in London Zoo's Reptile House.

'But that cuts across the holiday,' David was saying, a frown on his face.

'Yes, I know. That's what I wanted to tell you.'

'I remember reading something about it. Some kind of landslide, wasn't it?'

'The cliff broke off and fell on the village. There were fifteen dead. *The Chronicle Magazine* wants about three thousand words on how the people are coping; what difference it has made to their lives, a kind of chain reaction spreading out from the tragedy.'

'It sounds good. You'll go, of course.'

'I'd been looking forward to us going away.'

Simon came back. '*Dendroaspis polylepus*,' he said. 'The black mamba. Only it isn't really black, is it, Dad? More like the colour of black grapes with that white powder—'

'The bloom.'

'With the bloom still on them. A kind of greyish black, really.'

It was hard to imagine he was only nine. He was so grown up. David said it was from being by himself so much and reading everything he could lay his hands on.

When he'd gone back to the snakes David said, 'You're not worrying about me, are you?'

'No, of course not.'

'Because Simon and I will have a splendid holiday. We've been on our own before.'

'Yes. I know.'

She wanted him to say just two words: Darling. Come. And she would have dropped the story. But he was being so tremendously *reasonable*.

'I haven't said yes,' she said.

'But they're going to give you the lead, aren't they?'

'I suppose so. I'm not really bothered.'

'Of course you are. It'll be a terrific boost for you.'

'Couldn't you and Simon come down? I could work. We could see each other in the evenings.'

'But we've booked, darling. Paid for it. Anyway, Simon's crazy about beaches and the sea.'

'Dad! What does "reticulated" mean?' Simon said, pointing to a python.

'Diamond-patterned,' Alex said.

Simon continued to look at his father.

'Yes,' David said. 'That's right.'

The python slowly unwound. It had been fed a rat earlier that day and had constricted it in its coils. Now it released the dead, compressed body and started to swallow it.

'Come on,' David said hastily. 'Let's get out of here.'

They had tea but there was a sense of strain and tension and later, when David drove Alex back to her flat, he said, 'Darling, you do what you think best.'

He gave her a kiss on the cheek and got back into the car. She waved as they drove away and David raised a hand.

That night she made her decision. It had nothing to

do with the kudos which might accrue to her by leading a major magazine, nothing to do with the excitement of going out on a fascinating job, she decided to go because suddenly she wanted to think out her whole relationship with the man she loved. Or thought she loved.

4

Alex reached the Dordogne on a day which threatened rain and with a breeze puckering the surface of the river below Domme. She turned right along the north bank and, within a few minutes, Carriac was facing her on the far side of a long, sweeping bend. A mist was coming off the river and the houses, dressed in their yellow stone, were partly enshrouded, giving it the quality of a watercolour.

In the subdued light the cliffs above the village were a mixture of greys and fawns. The scar, where the collapse had occurred, was a raw off-white.

There was a sign on the outskirts in three languages telling her that her car was allowed no further. She parked and looked about her.

She had known Carriac, with its sister villages Beynac and La Roque-Gageac, since childhood. Her mother and father had had a long love affair with the river and she had played on its *plages* and swum in its heavy green water throughout her childhood.

They had stayed mostly at the Hôtel Bellevue and she could remember the lovely vine-shaded terrace overlooking the river where they had taken their meals on the hot summer evenings.

As she got out of her car another pulled up alongside. It was a Citroën from the 1950s, the *traction avant*, beautifully restored and painted a brilliant royal blue with burgundy leather upholstery and walnut fascia.

A young man got out and walked slowly towards the village. He, too, was from the 1950s, perhaps even from the 1920s. He wore a white suit with waistcoat, a long black macintosh draped from his shoulders and a white panama hat. He smoked a cigarette in a dark onyx holder. The whole effect was dramatic and stylish.

Alex opened the boot of her car, took from her camera bag a 200mm zoom and screwed it into the Nikon body. Then she walked slowly towards Carriac.

As she drew nearer she began to shoot pictures, knowing that most would have to be discarded. But she was of the Magnum school of photo-journalism: you shot and shot and shot and finally, from hundreds, you would choose fifty, then forty and so on until you might end up with half a dozen.

She photographed everything. The *gendarme*, the small queue at the PTT, the man who was putting rocks into a wheelbarrow and emptying them into the river, the cranes and the workmen on the cliff-top, the outline of the rear walls of houses against the cliff – all that was left to show they had once existed before being swept away.

She worked for more than half an hour, concentrating so intensely that she was unaware she was being watched. Slowly this grew on her as a feeling of discomfort and unease. She stopped and looked around.

The queue at the PTT was no longer waiting to go in but had come towards her. Five or six people with their baskets and baguettes stood watching her. A man in a khaki dust-coat further up the rubble at the base of the cliff had stopped whatever he was doing and had turned to look at her. The *gendarme* was looking and so was the young man from the 1950s illustration. Even the man who picked up the rubble had stopped.

It was as though the village had suddenly been struck dumb, turned to stone. But there was nothing lifeless about the expressions on the faces. Their mouths were tight, their eyes hostile.

The man in the khaki dust-coat came slowly down the slope of the rubble, picking his way between the larger slabs of rock. He was short and square with a heavy pock-marked face that would have been ugly had it not been for his bright blue eyes. He was in his fifties.

He stopped in front of her and, looking past her at her car with the GB sticker on the back, said in English, 'The camera. They do not like the camera.'

'Is photography forbidden?'

He shook his head gently. 'Not forbidden. Discouraged.' He had a strong accent which she knew was not French but which she could not place.

'Why?'

'This is where people died. Brothers, sisters, relatives, friends. It is not hard to understand.'

She had been in similar situations before. People were frequently too numb to object to the Press in the hours that followed a catastrophe. But later reaction set in and feelings of anger and grief synthesised into hatred of journalists.

There were two ways of reacting. The first was to tell them you were only doing your job and since there was no law against it you would continue. The second was emollient. Say you understood. Then come back later when there was no one around. Let them get used to you. Make friends. And she'd need to make friends if she was going to get a good background story to their present lives.

She chose the latter and turned away towards the hotel. She had been looking forward to the Bellevue.

The last time she had stayed there had been about ten years before, but she could clearly recall the cooking: the *friture de la Dordogne*, and, best of all, the crisply fried stuffed goose's neck.

She walked along the narrow path between the ruins and the river and came to the hotel.

It had never occurred to her that it too might have suffered. Now she saw that half the roof had gone and the workmen were busy putting up scaffolding.

The young man in the white suit and panama hat had been watching her from some distance away. He walked over and said, 'It is closed, but the bar and restaurant are still open.'

Her French was good but, taken by surprise, she did not register the words for a second.

'I beg . . . *Pardon?*'

'If you prefer I will speak English.'

She smiled and said in French, 'Whichever is easier for you.'

A flash of irritation seemed to fill his eyes and then it was gone. 'Your accent is excellent,' he said in English.

'Thank you.'

'May I offer you a drink?'

Here was a face that, if not friendly, did not seem actively hostile. 'Thank you. I could do with one.'

The terrace was untouched. The vine leaves were turning red and gold and the afternoon sun was driving away the rainy mist. She ordered a vermouth on the rocks.

'May I introduce myself? De Charny. You are a tourist?'

No use lying she thought. 'A journalist. A magazine journalist.'

This time a different look passed across his face.

'But everything has been written. We had all the Paris journalists. Radio. TV. What more is there?'

He spoke English perfectly with a trace of an American accent. He had removed his panama and his brown hair was very fine. He had a sallow face and wore gold-rimmed dark glasses.

'I'm interested in the aftermath rather than the event,' she said.

He pointed to the man with the wheelbarrow. 'Then you will be interested in Mijnheer van der Meulen. He cannot believe that his wife's body was found that night. He cannot accept that she is dead and buried with the others. So he goes on digging for her. He has been doing it every day since the tragedy. We are waiting to see what happens to him when he clears the site of his house and finds no one. It will be interesting.'

She wanted to make notes, to ask questions, but she thought: if I come on too strong I'll frighten him away and he's all I've got.

'Do they . . . ' – she indicated the village as a whole – 'Do they resent the Press?'

'Naturally.'

'And they would like me to go away?'

'I think that is true.'

'Well, I have a job to do. And, as the saying goes, it's a free country.'

'Freedom demands responsibility,' he said.

She finished her drink in one long swallow. The last thing she wanted was a lecture on civics.

There was a sudden roaring noise and a young man dressed in a long black leather coat, black leather leggings and a black helmet, pulled up beneath the terrace on a powerful motorcycle.

Her companion excused himself and went over. The two spoke briefly, the throbbing of the bike's engine making it impossible for her to hear anything. The motorcyclist gave her a quick searching look. Then he turned the bike and went racing away up the road.

'I must be getting along,' she said.

'Where will you stay?'

'There are other hotels.'

'I think you will find them full.'

'Oh?'

'If you look around the village you will see that most of the houses are empty. And they will remain so until the dynamiting is finished. The families have been placed in hotels. There are no spare beds anywhere.'

'I hadn't realised—'

'I have an idea. If you would like to stay here I know of a house. I could make a call.'

She could think of nothing better. To be in a house belonging to the village would give her much of the background she would need. 'I'd be very grateful,' she said.

He rose, bowed slightly, and went indoors to the telephone.

5

The house was a mixture of styles: French château, with a touch of Scottish baronial. It stood just outside the village behind a high Cupressus hedge. It was surrounded by trees: oaks, monkey puzzles, walnuts and horse chestnuts. There were shrubberies and great banks of rhododendrons and azaleas near the road, and parts of the garden were overgrown by bamboos. Even on a day in high summer it gave the impression of being not only damp but dank.

Mary Corton worked in a tower on the northern side of the building. When she had originally bought the house it was the tower that had appealed to her. Away from the sound of the telephone, it would separate her from her family; it would enable her to write in peace. That was the theory.

She'd lived to regret it. Firstly, the tower was round and she had to have all her furniture – her desk, her tables, even her book-cases – made to fit it.

She did not, of course, have a telephone in the tower but that had not stopped her hearing it ring in other parts of the house. And when it rang she wanted to know who was on the other end, especially if it was one of Georges' conquests.

Now, as she sat in front of her word processor, she thought she could hear it ringing.

'I can't go on like this!' she said out loud, and

for the hundredth time considered having her room sound-proofed.

The ringing stopped. She concentrated on her writing. She read the preceding sentence:

'*Oh, my darling, do you know how much I need you? Want you?*' Lord Harry said.
'*I am below your station,*' Charlotte replied.
'*Damn my station!*' his lordship cried, crushing her to him.

Her fingers hovered over the keys for some moments. It was not often 'Susanna Bellairs' had to think for long. Her novels 'wrote themselves' – or at least that's what she told her friends. In reality, of course, she worked eight hours a day every day. But in spite of the hard work her recent sales figures were down.

Her standing orders were that she was never to be disturbed by the telephone during working hours. But how was she to find out who was phoning if she wasn't disturbed?

She rose and stood at the window, looking out over rounded hills. The walnut trees were beginning to turn and she could see the yellow tobacco leaves in the fields. Soon they would be hanging in the airing barns. She nibbled at the quick of her nail. Was Georges at it again?

Not that she particularly wanted him back in her bedroom. She couldn't stand his night table with all its pills and creams and unguents that were meant to keep him young. If only his mistresses could see him then! No, it wasn't that. It was the humiliation. The last time she had felt the stares, cringed at the little smiles half hidden behind hands. She did not want that again and she'd told him so. Once more and he was out for good.

She looked at herself in a long mirror behind the door. She was small and trim but there was no gainsaying the grey hair near her ears. Her face was still reasonable though her neck was beginning to go. Always the first sign, she thought bitterly.

None of 'Susanna Bellairs'' heroines ever had wrinkles. They never had impure thoughts, either. Sometimes she wondered what they did, all these beautiful virgins, once they were off her pages. All the Charlottes and Josephines and Catrionas and Isabellas.

She knew where some of them went. They popped up in thick novels by 'Serena Susskind' and had their bodices ripped off and their knickers pulled down and, as Max had observed, 'Got good and properly screwed.'

Well, there was no point in wasting plots was there?

The phone call still bothered her. She went down the narrow stair-case that led from the tower and along the first-floor landing. The thud...thud...thud...of heavy rock was coming from Neville's room. She'd asked him a hundred times to keep it down, but that was something she could no longer insist upon.

His door was open and his wheelchair was where it always was these days, facing the window that looked out over the river, its back to the room.

When he'd returned from hospital with the newspaper cuttings and the word 'hero' ringing in his ears they had tried to turn his bedroom into a sitting-room by day and a bedroom by night, to give him a change of scene. But he had quickly turned it into his usual pit. Between the junk were paths on which he could steer the wheelchair...to the TV...to the window...to the stereo...and back...

The television was on now, with the sound turned down. Above the rock she could hear the plink-plonk ...plink-plonk of the electronic game which obsessed him. It was a small screen he could hold on his lap and the game comprised three manikins that fell into rivers unless you were quick enough on the button to get a bridge there first. It was the one thing he could do superbly.

She knocked on the door so she would not startle him. He did not react. She put her hand on his shoulder and felt him flinch.

'Can I get you anything, darling?'

He did not reply. The manikins went round and round. She remembered vividly – would never forget as long as she lived – the hours he was trapped. He'd been covered by dust and rubble and the rock slabs had threatened to shift and crush him every second. She'd held his hand and talked and talked, trying to keep his mind off himself and the dead body that lay beside him, trying to stop him from giving up and dying.

'You're a hero,' she had said. 'Just remember that. A real hero.'

Once, she'd given up her place to Georges and he had sat on the rubble with Neville as they waited for the crane to arrive. She thought her son would have wanted that but he seemed worse when she came back. That was the first moment she had registered his frozen silence. Before that there had been tears. Then only this frozen silence.

She came to the front of the wheelchair. He was beginning to put on weight. The specialist had warned her about that, too. His face was pudgy. She remembered him best as a thin-faced little boy.

Those were the days when they had been very close; unified against his father, Les. She hadn't thought of Les for a long time but when her mind revived the picture of Neville as a child it revived Les, too: violent, drunken

Les. He hadn't cared who he was hitting – Mary or Neville – so long as he was hitting *someone*.

It was no wonder Neville had been sickly and introverted; no wonder he had started by hating his stepfather even though Georges' charm was legendary. Now, at nineteen, he was neither youth nor adult, but that peculiar stage in between.

'Would you like something to read?' she said.

Plink-plonk . . . Plink-plonk . . .

It was no use.

'I'll look in again,' she said, and went off in search of Georges.

She found him in his study where he 'worked'. It was a room she did not often visit because it depressed her, with its dark, brooding atmosphere.

The walls were lined with book-cases in which there were editions – every edition Georges could lay his hands upon – of the *Almanach de Gotha*, *Burke's Peerage* and *Debrett's*.

Against one wall, was a pair of crossed lances. In a glass cabinet were the helm, greaves, and breastplate of a knight of the Middle Ages. There were wall charts of genealogical tables and family trees with their heraldic devices. Above the door hung a shield (reproduction) bearing the device of five horizontal bands, pointed, of red on white, or, as Georges liked to describe it, 'Barry of five, vair and gules.' And behind his ornate desk a red banner, above which were the words: MONTJOIE – ST DENIS!

On his desk were several volumes of Froissart's *Chroniques* and he was taking notes.

He rose as Mary entered the room. He was tall, and dressed with immaculate care in a double-breasted blazer with brass buttons on which he had had stamped the Corton crest. He was wearing a club tie which Mary did not recognise, but that did not surprise her, for he was a member of more clubs than anyone she had ever met. His white shirt was of the finest sea island cotton which he had made by Sulka in Paris. He looked expensive and was. She knew for she paid for it all.

He was a pear-shaped man with a pink, shiny skin, and soft delicate hands.

'*Chérie!*' He came round the desk and took her hand. 'You look ravishing this morning!'

'Thank you.'

He paid this kind of grandiloquent compliment to every woman he met.

'How are you getting on with your researches?' she said, more to start the conversation than for any interest she had.

'Splendidly.' He spoke English perfectly, with only a slight French accent. His women loved the accent.

He touched the hair near his neck and absentmindedly rubbed his fingers together. She knew that he had been having recourse to the Grecian 2000 – there was not a grey hair on his head.

She had met him soon after she had divorced Les and had been swept off her feet. He had been living in England then and worked in PR – something to do with the promotion of French cheese. The moment they married he had abandoned his job and taken up his 'research'.

This, in reality, meant trying to establish his own line of descent from Sire de Corton, a Norman knight of the fourteenth century, and agitating in the local and national press for a return of a king to the French throne.

She had not minded his indolence and vanity in the beginning, for he gave her the kind of background that she, a suburban girl from Brighton, could have only dreamed about. It was a background, too, that she needed for her work: all those Lord Harrys and Comtes de Whatsits. Georges knew their backgrounds and foregrounds and everything about them.

'Neville's just as bad today,' she said.

'Ah.'

'When do you take him for his next physio?'

'Tomorrow.'

'See if you can get him to make more of an effort.'

'Of course.'

She paused, waiting, but Georges resumed his seat at the desk. Finally she said, 'The phone call, Georges. Was it for me?'

His eyes slid away. 'No, *chérie*, I meant to tell you. It was Derek.'

Derek was Neville's friend. 'I wish he'd come to see Neville.'

'Why should he? Neville won't speak to him. Or to Pierre. You can't expect them to go on trying.'

'They were such friends!'

'They have their own lives.'

'He feels it, you know. I can tell.'

'That's why I said yes.'

She frowned, uncomprehending.

'To Derek. There is a young Englishwoman in the village. A journalist. She was going to stay at the hotel, but of course that is impossible. So Derek said he would phone us.'

'About what?'

'About a room, *chérie*. She has nowhere to stay.'

'Georges, are you mad?'

'Listen, my love. She is a journalist writing for a big magazine. These people find out things.'

'What sort of things?'

'Just things. It is better that she does it here, under our eyes.'

'Georges—'

'I was in PR remember. Any more publicity – I mean bad publicity, especially in England – and the village can say goodbye to next season and the one after that. And if there are no visitors from Britain to spend their pounds there will be no seasons after that for many of our friends.'

'Since when did you give a damn about the village?'

'Darling, you wound me.'

She ignored that. 'Anyway, what can we do about it?'

'Mould her. Show her the positive side. Show her what everyone is doing to make this not only the most beautiful but the safest village on the river.'

What was he up to?

'And,' Georges went on, 'she is young. It will give Neville an interest.'

There had to be more to it than that, she thought. He was lying. Why? Had he met this creature before? Was she another of his conquests pretending to be a journalist?

Then she suddenly thought: why not? Just her presence might cause a reaction in Neville. And anything that gave him a chance was to be encouraged.

Georges listened to Mary go back up the stairs into the tower. He rose and took a slender parcel from behind the door and went along the corridor to Neville's room.

'Bonjour, Neville.' He turned the wheelchair so that when he sat on Neville's bed it faced him.

Neville looked at him with wary eyes. Georges was always making little private visits these days.

'I've brought something very special for you,' Georges said. He unwrapped the parcel and displayed a double-handed sword. He held it up before him so that the handle looked like a cross, and then he kissed it. 'It is for you,' he said.

It was the one thing Neville had wanted more than any other. But now he did not react.

'It might have been used at the Battle of Poitiers. It might even have been used by the Count of Dammartin. It is nice to believe so, don't you think?'

He placed the sword on Neville's lap. 'Hold it.'

But the hands drew away.

'As you know, in those days they swore on their swords. I want you to think about that.' He rose. 'I'll put it over here.' He leaned the sword against the wall. 'But above all they were faithful to the king. Don't forget that. One day you will speak again. One day you will want to tell the truth. But only to me, Neville. Only to me! Do you understand?'

He paused, staring at the crippled figure, then said, 'I nearly forgot. A young woman is coming to stay. An English journalist. She has come to write a story about the village.'

As he left, the wariness in Neville's eyes was replaced by fear.

6

The first-floor terrace of the Hôtel Bellevue was a grape arbour with a view of the river below. Alex thought it one of the most romantic spots she had ever seen. She walked up the stone steps in the warm dusk and imagined the evening ahead if David had been there. The place was almost deserted. There was only one diner, the middle-aged man with the pock-marked face and bright blue eyes who had spoken to her about taking photographs earlier that afternoon.

He was sitting at one end of a row of tables nearest the river. She made for one at the other end.

As she was pulling out a chair a small, elderly woman, with her hair drawn back in a bun and a severe expression on her face, hurried over from the kitchen and said, 'We are not open!'

Alex had had a long, tiring day. She recognised the woman as one of a legion of female restaurant managers who, over the years, sometimes coldly, sometimes with pale warmth, had shown her to tables all over France.

She paused before sitting down. 'You are clearly open.'

'I mean we do not have a proper menu.'

'I don't mind. Just an omelette.'

The woman stared at her and was about to produce another objection when Alex said, 'Unless, of course, you wish me to go to the *syndicat d'initiative* in Sarlat and ask why some people are served but not others.'

The woman closed her mouth with a snap, then said, 'This table is for four people. Please follow me.'

She led Alex to a table on the far side of the terrace where there was no view of the river, then began to fuss with table-cloth and cutlery.

Alex was about to ask why the other diner was at a table for four, but the adrenalin had drained from her.

'I will bring you the menu,' the woman said.

As she left, the man rose and came over to her, bowed and said, 'My name is Dr Wellmann.' He pronounced the 'w' as a 'v' in the German way. 'Max Wellmann. We met this afternoon.'

Alex introduced herself and they shook hands. 'You cannot see the river from this dark place,' he said. 'May I have the pleasure of your company?'

By the time the woman returned Alex was seated at Max Wellmann's table, looking down on the slippery green body of water flowing silently past.

'It is all right, Madame Corbie,' he said. 'I will see she does not steal the cutlery.'

Alex ordered a tomato salad and then a ham and mushroom omelette.

Dr Wellmann said, 'Allow me to buy the wine.' He ordered a Bordeaux from the Côtes de Castillon.

'Does everyone here dislike me?' she said.

'They're suspicious. This village depends on tourists. They're scared of what you're going to publish.'

'You can tell them that *The Chronicle Magazine* isn't the *Reader's Digest*. It's not going to make much difference.'

'*The Chronicle*? It's a paper I've always admired.'

'I'm surprised you've heard of it.'

'I used to write for it.'

'That's amazing! When?'

'When you were still at school. It's a long story. But tell me, where are you staying?'

'The Cortons'.'

His bushy eyebrows shot up. 'That's strange. I would have thought . . . ' He stopped.

'The young man in the panama hat and white suit arranged it.'

'Blackwood?'

'I thought he said his name was de Charny.'

'No, no, that's Derek Blackwood.'

'That's what Monsieur Corton said.' She remembered his sudden flash of anger. 'I must have misheard.'

'Do you remember a French actress called Julia Berri?' She shook her head.

'No, before your time. She was well known in France, mainly for marrying. I think she had five husbands. Derek was the product of an American father. Part of his childhood was spent in Hollywood.'

The omelette came and she ate hungrily. He did not interrupt but sipped his wine. When she had finished she mopped up what was left on the plate with a piece of bread and popped it into her mouth.

He nodded his approval. 'The best mouthful.'

'This is what you dream about on cold, winter Sundays.' Then, 'Why were you surprised to hear I was staying at the Cortons'?'

'Because of the son, Neville. It seems a strange time to take in a visitor.'

'I thought so myself.'

The three of them had been on the terrace when she had arrived. Georges was shaking dry Martinis but she had accepted a glass of wine instead. They went through the niceties: how grateful Alex was; and from Georges, about not wanting her to get the wrong impression of the village. Mary had drawn her out about England and asked her if she knew Brighton. Neville had not spoken at all.

They had had their drinks surrounded by large terracotta pots filled with fuchsias and pelargoniums and the air had been heavy with warmth and moisture. She had sensed a strain and once or twice had tried to draw Neville into the conversation by directing a question or a remark in his direction. He had simply stared back at her.

'I had the feeling they were representing the village,' she said to Wellmann. 'Kind of lords of the manor.'

He chuckled. 'That's how Georges sees himself. I suppose you've heard of Mary. Her books are well known in England.'

'She mentioned something about it. I've seen the names, of course. Tell me about Neville. He never spoke a word while I was there.'

'He hasn't spoken since that night. That's how we describe it now. Just "that night". He was trying to save the life of one of our village characters, a little hunchback called Petit Louis. A wall collapsed on them. It killed Petit Louis and – well, you've seen Neville.'

'I've always been terrified of paraplegia.'

'There's nothing physically wrong with him. His mother's had dozens of X-rays taken. It's caused by trauma. He spent hours under the rocks and there were beams on top of him. The beams saved him. But the stones were unbalanced. At any moment they could have shifted and crushed him to death.'

'How long will it take him to get over it?'

'One never knows with trauma.'

'Are you their doctor?'

'No, I haven't practised for years.'

He ordered another bottle of wine. It grew dark and

the lights of the restaurant were reflected in the black, shiny water, rolling silently to the sea.

They talked about the night of the tragedy and she began to wish she had come prepared with her notebook.

'Perhaps it was *because* of Neville they took you in,' he said. 'Something to break the pattern. He won't even see his old friends. There were three of them – Neville and Derek and another young man called Pierre Chervas, whose father is a wealthy businessman in Souillac.'

She remembered the young man on the powerful motorcycle, and mentioned him.

'That's Pierre. They were like the three musketeers. Always together. Now Neville won't see either Derek or Pierre.'

'What does he do, the step-father?'

'Nothing. Georges believes work is demeaning. He spends his time in the fourteenth century. He would have been happier then. A knight perhaps, but better still, the king.'

As they paid their bills he said, 'You've saved me from a very dull evening.'

'And you've been fascinating.'

'Let me escort you back to the house.' The word 'escort' had an almost Victorian ring to it.

They walked along the dark, deserted *quai*, then took the path through the rubble. The Dutchman's wheelbarrow and spade stood in the darkness, ready for the morrow.

At the Cortons' drive he said, 'Come and see me tomorrow. There are things . . . ' He paused. He seemed to be about to say something further then changed his mind. 'Perhaps I can give you some help. One journalist to another.'

★

The house blazed with light as Alex walked up the drive and it reminded her of a great liner putting out to sea. The big drawing-room was empty and she went up the stairs to her room. The corridor branched left and right. Her room was right but as she reached the landing she heard the sound of voices to her left.

She paused. It was only one voice. Mary Corton's. 'Darling, you've got to try,' she was saying. Her words were soft and the anguish was plain enough. 'You're young. You've got your whole life ahead of you. We'll do everything we can but you've got to make the effort...'

Alex turned away and tiptoed to her own room, locking the door behind her. She wondered if Max Wellmann was right. Was that why they had invited her into their home? To break the pattern?

Her suitcase was on the bed. The moment she opened it she felt the contents had been displaced. She had never been a neat packer and this looked too neat for her. Had someone opened it, looked through the contents and then repacked it?

Wait. Hang on, she thought. That way led paranoia. She tried to recall what the contents had looked like the last time she had repacked it on the Channel ferry. Had she taken extra care? Perhaps she had packed more neatly than usual. Perhaps this was just her imagination stemming from a mixture of tiredness and strangeness and the awareness of the village's hostility.

She sat for a while in an easy chair, making notes of her conversation with Dr Wellmann. She was in the middle of a sentence, the point of her pen raised, when she heard footsteps coming softly along the corridor. They paused outside her door. She waited for them to continue but they did not. She rose, crossed silently to the door and put her ear to it. She thought she could hear someone breathing. In the movies people wrenched open the door at this point and the person on the other side toppled into the room. After a few moments there was the faintest creak of a floorboard and the footsteps continued along the passage.

Probably just making sure I was in for the night, she told herself with more optimism than she felt.

She got ready for bed and went into the bathroom. It was lit by moonlight and she spent some moments trying to find the light switch. In the semi-darkness she stubbed her foot against the bidet and, cursing silently, held on to the basin while she rubbed it.

The bathroom window was directly above the basin and was partially open. She realised that the bathroom was at an angle to the middle section of the house, for its window looked directly on to Neville's room. She could see him in his wheelchair, lit by the blue-green phosphorescence of the television screen.

He was looking down at something on his lap, in great concentration.

Plink-plonk . . . plink-plonk . . .

The three manikins circled endlessly round the electronic screen. But Neville was no longer playing. Although he was staring into the screen he was really seeing Petit Louis just as he had after the wall collapsed.

The picture was crisply clear in his mind. He had thought him dead. But then, through the dust, he had seen the little hunchback dragging himself over the jagged masonry. He had been coming towards Neville. The top and side of his head was pulpy and blood was pouring down his face. He looked like an animal, not human at all. He heaved himself along like a stumpy, legless alligator.

Neville could not move. The beams were holding up the rock. One tiny movement and great slabs would teeter and fall.

He was trapped. He knew what was going to happen. Petit Louis was going to kill him. He opened his mouth to scream . . .

Was that the dream? Or was it the reality?

He sat in his wheelchair, feeling the sweat run down his chest.

His heart said: God help me. His mind said: why should He?

He wanted comfort.

And then he remembered the sword. He had placed it in his special cupboard, the one no one but he might open. He took out the keys and wheeled himself to it. He glanced at the door of his room. It was shut. He opened the cupboard and took out the sword. He held it before him and kissed the blade.

'I swear . . . ' he began. 'I swear . . . '

He felt the tears now at the back of his eyes.

'I swear . . . '

But swear what? And to whom?

From her viewpoint in the bathroom Alex watched him press the hilt against his forehead.

7

The morning sun was hot and the air filled with the sound of rock drills at the top of the cliffs. The *gendarme* was in his place with his walkie-talkie. Shoppers were moving from one end of the village to the other along the path through the rubble. And Thomas van der Meulen was already at work, filling his wheelbarrow with stones, trundling them down to the river's edge and tipping them into the water. Even though they were not big and the river was deep and strong, it was possible to see a mound of stones growing larger and larger beneath the surface.

Alex had spent ten minutes watching the Dutchman. She had photographed him from various angles. He was tall and cadaverous, wearing espadrilles, a pair of dark trousers that had once belonged to a city suit, and a collarless shirt.

He was already at work by the time she arrived and was now covered in pale grey dust. She finished the roll of film and put it in the camera bag. She always kept her new film in a separate compartment. It was empty. She rummaged among the lenses and camera bodies but there was no new film at all.

It was one of her regular checks before going on a job. But had she done it this time? She couldn't remember. It was like the suitcase. You did things without necessarily having them imprinted on your brain for ever.

A shadow fell across her and she looked up. The Dutchman was standing above her, his face knotted by anger. 'Why do you do this?' he said.

'I'm sorry. I don't under—'

'Leave me alone. This is a grave. Do you not understand that? You people are like vultures!'

He walked slowly back to his wheelbarrow, leaving Alex shaken. She picked up the camera bag and went off in search of film.

Once, there had been a small *presse*, part of its façade was still standing, but the rest had gone. She looked along the village street and in the distance saw a postcard display outside the small *supermarché*. It had a single check-out above which were shelves of cigarettes and films.

A dozen people were in the shop and she joined the queue. She was still upset by the ferocity of van der Meulen's attack and all her antennae were bristling.

A middle-aged woman at the cash register said, 'We have none,' when Alex asked her for film.

'Behind you,' Alex said, pointing.

The woman said, 'It is old stock.'

'How old?'

'Out of date.'

'May I see?'

The woman now looked at her fully for the first time. 'It is not for sale. It must go back to the wholesalers.' She spoke slowly as though to a child.

'I don't *believe* this!' Alex said in English and turned to look at the others in the shop. But they were studiously looking away, fascinated by tins and packets.

Furious, she went out into the hot sunlight and thought: to hell with them. She decided to go into Sarlat. She slung her camera bag over her shoulder and went off down the *quai* to the little car park shaded by plane-trees.

Her white Golf was sandwiched between a blue van and a Renault. She opened the boot, put in the camera bag, slammed it closed and was about to open the door when she saw that one of the front tyres was flat. She might have picked up a nail on the way down. But somehow she did not think so.

For the first time a shadow of fear passed quickly over her like a sudden chilly breeze on a warm summer's day.

From the other side of the Renault a voice said, 'Good morning. Did you sleep well?'

She looked up and saw Max Wellman. 'I've got a flat,' she said. 'And I've got to go into Sarlat and get some film. Is there a taxi?'

'There's a small garage in the village. I know the mechanic. I'll tell him to come and fix your tyre. Meantime, I'm going into Sarlat myself. It will be a pleasure to have some company.'

They drove along the river for a couple of kilometres and then swung inland.

'How are your hosts today?' he said.

'Fine . . . I think. I haven't seen them this morning.'

'Mary starts work early. And Georges gets up late.'

The maid had brought her coffee and brioche at eight o'clock. She had looked out of her bathroom window again but Neville's window was closed. She decided not to tell Max Wellmann what she had seen. Now, in the bright sunlight, it seemed so bizarre she wondered if she had not imagined it.

'When did you write for *The Chronicle*?' she said, picking up his statement of the day before.

'I started in Vienna,' he said. 'My father was the owner of a small anti-fascist newspaper. I grew up with the smell of hot metal and wet page proofs. We knew *The Chronicle*'s correspondent in Vienna. When he was out of town I covered for him. I started to write for *The Chronicle* when I was doing my medical studies at university in the nineteen-fifties. You remember a movie called *The Third Man?*'

'Of course.'

'The first piece I ever wrote for them was called "Looking for Harry Lime". It was a picture of Vienna after the Russians pulled out in the mid-fifties.

'The year after I took my medical degree my father died and I took over the paper. I had always wanted to do that. Medicine was my mother's idea. A good Jewish mother always likes to say, "My son, the doctor." ' He smiled to himself.

'So you never practised?'

'A bit, in the Argentine.'

They were driving through the rich leafy countryside. 'I'm surprised an anti-fascist newspaper was needed in Vienna after the war.'

'It's not just a city of Sachertorte and Rosenkavalier. Vienna was as fascist as anywhere else. More so. It is deep inside us. A legacy of the Hapsburgs.'

'Why did you go to the Argentine?'

'My wife was Argentinian. She was always homesick for Buenos Aires. She couldn't live in Vienna. So eventually I said, all right, let's go back, let's try it for a while.'

'I'd kept abreast of medicine, reading the journals, that sort of thing. So I put up my brass plate. But I suppose the old itch was there. I mean for an anti-fascist platform. Vienna seemed almost left-wing by comparison with Buenos Aires. It was the time of the Generals.

'I started a small weekly newspaper and began writing again for *The Chronicle* in London.

'Of course we got threatening letters and phone calls.

The usual thing. We had a son then, Friedrich. He was twenty-two and mildly left-wing, like a lot of the young people. And one day he just disappeared. He was on his way to the university, on a little motor scooter. Nothing was ever seen of him again. The scooter was thrown over our wall.

'That finished my wife and it nearly finished me. She became one of the Mothers of the Lost Ones.'

'I've seen them on TV.'

'I don't think she wanted to live after Friedrich disappeared and a year later she died. I sold my practice. There was some money from her side of the family and I came back to Europe. I couldn't face Vienna so I came down here. Now you know all about me.'

In Sarlat Alex went to a photographic shop, handed in her exposed film and bought a new supply, all the while wondering why he had told her, why he had been so frank, when everyone else in the village was just the opposite.

She did some shopping and they met for a drink at one of the cafés below the cathedral walls. The close familiarity of the car had gone and he chatted inconsequentially.

Then, abruptly, he leaned across the table and said, 'It was those articles I wrote for *The Chronicle* that killed Friedrich. I wrote about fascism, about the death squads, about the Generals. And they marked us. One day they took him to show they were stronger than we were, that the sword was mightier than the pen.'

'Why have you told me all this?'

'Why? I don't know. Maybe it is because you work for *The Chronicle* too. Maybe it is because it is the only newspaper I ever trusted except my own. Maybe . . . '

He stopped and his face changed. The humour in his

eyes, which was a feature of his face, was wiped out. 'Come,' he said. 'I want to show you something.'

Georges Corton parked his wife's large Mercedes at the end of an overgrown lane and stepped fastidiously along the grassy edge so that his Gucci loafers did not pick up mud from the deep wheel tracks. At the end of the lane stood the mill and he could already hear the sound of the mill-race.

Parts of the mill dated from the fifteenth century. It was built beside one of the clear streams that rush down the slope of the hills to join the Dordogne above Carriac. For years it had been occupied by an English couple who had done it up in 'Home Counties' cottage' style but recently they had sold it to Derek Blackwood, who was in the process of undoing it.

It was a beautiful old place, standing alone in three hectares of oak and grassland. Georges paused and looked at the grey stone of the building and the sun dappling through the oak leaves and thought that it could not have changed in four hundred years. No telegraph pole could be seen, no pylon, and the mill-race blocked the noise of traffic from the road half a kilometre away.

At the side of the house was a large, flagged terrace built over the mill-race itself, and from its stone balustrade he looked down into the clear waters of the mill pond directly on to the backs of two large trout which lay finning at the base of the flume.

He banged on the oak front door and called, 'Derek!'

Above the noise of the rushing water he heard Derek's voice call, 'In here!'

The mill looked bigger from the outside than it was inside, for the walls were massive. Georges went into the living-room which overlooked the mill pond. The water lapped against the walls of the house just below the windows so that he had the sensation of being almost at water level.

The walls, which had once been lined with plaster-board and paper, had been put back to their original state: huge grey slabs of stone, fitting so snugly together that they hardly needed mortar for the joints.

The great fire-place, which in winter would burn logs the size of a sheep, had been rescued from chintzed seats and horse-brasses. Derek stood at the window and looked out over the water. He was dressed in pale grey herring-bone of the best worsted.

Georges said, 'Coming down the lane I couldn't see a single symbol of the twentieth century. It could have been Aquitaine.'

Derek was smoking a cigarette in his onyx holder and he looked at Georges now through his gold-rimmed, dark glasses. 'You're a romantic. You've been one ever since I first knew you.'

There was something patronising in the way he said it and Georges had to remind himself that Derek was no longer the boy who used to come and play with Neville and who had sat at his feet listening avidly to tales of battle. He had grown up; he was a man.

'Isn't it going to be a bit cold in winter?' Georges said, thinking of the gales which would be caused by the huge fire-place.

Derek ignored him. 'I'm going to have rushes on the floor and sconces on the walls.' He pointed to the metal-framed windows. 'They're obscene! This room needs leaded lattice-windows. And I'll find a real iron spit for the fire-place.'

'And don't forget the dented pewter tankards,' Georges said, with irony. He was not yet willing for the pupil to take over from his master.

'Don't be too clever, Georges, it doesn't suit you.'

A year ago he would never have spoken to him like that, but Georges decided not to make an issue of it.

'What about the journalist?' Derek said.

'What about her?'

'What is she after?'

'What are all journalists after?'

'I thought it better that she went to someone like you. I mean, one doesn't want one-sided stories.'

'No, one doesn't, does one?'

'How's Neville?'

'The same.'

'Has he spoken yet?'

'No.'

Derek looked at him sharply. 'I never thought of him as a hero.'

'No one did.'

'We'd like to come and visit him.'

'I've told you before. It's not possible.'

'Why not?'

'Visits upset him.'

'How do you know if he can't speak?'

'Maybe later. We'll see what happens. Who knows, the journalist may be a blessing in disguise. The psychologist said there was a kind of log jam in his mind. Once that is broken all the memories will come pouring out and he'll be well again.'

'I could help,' Derek said. 'I'm part of his background.'

'I don't mean those memories. We're all part of those. I mean that night. Another few seconds and he would have freed Petit Louis and dragged him out and both would still be alive. You know, I always wondered . . .'

'What?'

'What Petit Louis was doing there. He doesn't live

in the village. It was after midnight. The bars were closed.'

'It doesn't really matter now, does it? He's dead.'

'But it matters to us. Neville is alive, you see. And it matters because of who we are. As you say, Neville is an unlikely hero. But his rescue was the action of Sire de Charny, don't you think?'

Derek looked away.

'Why did you call yourself that to her?'

'Did I?'

'She says you did.'

'What if I did?'

'Is that how you see yourself? The perfect knight?'

'Perhaps.'

'It was a *game* Derek. Something between us. Something special.'

'I don't think of it as a game!' His face was suddenly cold.

The two men looked at each other in silence for a few seconds. Then, above the noise of the mill-race, they heard the throb of a motorcycle. It stopped, and a moment or two later Pierre Chervas came into the mill. He was dressed in his long, black leather coat, black leggings and black helmet. He looked to Georges like some sinister spaceman.

He was a year or two older than Neville. Big and muscular. Georges had always found him unimaginative but he and Derek were close.

'I must go,' Georges said abruptly.

The other two watched him through the window as he made his way up the lane. Then Chervas said, 'What did he want?'

'He's sniffing around.'

'You think he's putting it together?'

'How the Christ do I know?' He pushed another

cigarette into his holder and snapped his lighter. 'So what's new?'

'The journalist was unlucky. She had a flat tyre. I think she's beginning to get the picture.'

'And?'

'She went into Sarlat with Dr Max.'

'Why?'

'I dunno. I followed them in but all they did was shopping and have a drink.'

'And then?'

'Then I came back here.'

'What did I tell you?'

'You told me to check on her. See what she was doing. That's what I—'

'God damn it! What about after they left Sarlat? We don't know where they went or what they did.'

'I'm telling you! It was just a little shopping trip.'

'Christ, don't you understand! She's not like the others. She's got time. She's not in a rush. She can dig and dig.'

'She won't find anything,' Pierre said. 'Because there's nothing to find.'

8

Dr Wellmann turned off the main Sarlat-Carriac road and took a smaller road down to the Dordogne. The countryside grew more dense and they passed a broken-down cottage with a lorry parked at the back.

'That was Petit Louis' place,' he said. 'The hunchback Neville tried to save.' He slowed down and almost came to a halt. The door was shut and the windows covered on the inside by newspapers brown with age.

'He was like someone out of a fairytale. A troll from the depths of the forest. But powerful. I've seen him unload a pile of heavy logs from his lorry in a few minutes. Yet his hobby was bird photography. He took beautiful pictures. He submitted them to the *salon* in Périgueux and almost always won a prize.'

A little further on Max opened a gate and drove up to a house which had been built on the bank of the river.

The place was a ruin. At one time it must have been attractive, Alex thought, with a breathtaking view upstream to Carriac. Now only the shell remained. Blackened timbers lay in piles along one wall. The roof was gone. One gable had toppled to the ground, the other was open to the sky. Torn wallpaper flapped in the breeze, and the paintwork was stained by smoke and fire. The garden was becoming rank.

She got out of the car and followed as Max walked slowly to the gaping hole where the front door had once been.

'Careful where you tread,' he said.

Some of the floorboards were charred, others missing, and there was still a smell of burning in the warm, humid air even though the fire had clearly occurred some time before.

She followed him in. Some walls were intact, others had fallen. There were pieces of broken furniture and stained carpets everywhere.

'This is our other tragedy,' he said. 'It happened in early summer.'

He moved a piece of timber and they went further into the ruin.

'It was a pretty house. Not old, but built of the local stone. I knew the owners. A nice English couple called Harris. They were from London. He had been an accountant with one of the big oil companies. They were both in their seventies. This was their summer home. They came out in May every year – except this year, when they arrived in April.' He bent down suddenly, lifted an empty bottle, sniffed at it and put it back.

'On the night of their arrival the house caught fire and they were killed.'

Again Alex wondered why he was telling her this.

'The official view is that their deaths were caused by an exploding gas cylinder.'

'I've read about cases like that.'

'They're not uncommon. Especially here in France where everyone uses gas. Everyone, that is, except Mr and Mrs Harris.'

He stopped and there was a moment of silence. She said, 'What do you mean?'

'Pieces of a thirty-kilo gas cylinder were found after the fire. But I've been here many times and I never saw a gas appliance, a heater, a stove, or anything else. The house was all electric.'

She frowned. 'Don't people keep them as spares in the country in case of power-cuts? I know my father did when we lived in the country.'

'That's what the police said.'

'But you don't think so.'

'All my . . . what do you call them? All my "feelers" tell me it wasn't so. Look, have you ever tried to lift a thirty-kilo gas cylinder?'

'No.'

'They're heavy. Mrs Harris had arthritis of the hands. Mr Harris had disc trouble in his back. Neither could have lifted a gas cylinder.'

'If it wasn't an accident then what was it? You're not seriously suggesting . . . ' She stared at him for a moment then said, 'You told the police all this? I mean your theories?'

'Of course. They said thank you very much and did nothing. They don't like what they think are simple things made complicated, especially where foreigners are concerned.'

'Let me get it clear. Are you telling me you think this was deliberate? Because if that's so then—'

'That's right. It would be murder.'

The word hung in the smoke-tainted air like some noisome thing he had disinterred from the ruins.

'But *why*?'

'Let's get away from here.'

They walked down to the river where a punt, half filled with water, was moored to the bank.

He said, 'Where I come from such violence is not unheard of. That's why I say all my feelers were out.

'My father used to tell me stories of house-burnings in the Austrian countryside before the war. They were mostly owned by Jews.

'Then in the Argentine I found that your house

could be fire-bombed merely for telling the truth. In Wales, you can get your holiday house burned down for being English.'

She said, 'But the French have never done things like that. They've got a marvellous tradition of letting foreigners live in their country. You're living here yourself and the English have been living here for centuries.'

'Don't be fooled by that. There is a dark side to the French. They have a National Front much bigger than the one in England. You only have to listen to Monsieur le Pen.'

'What do the police say?'

'They say many houses burned down last winter. In Périgord alone more than thirty.'

'And you're telling me because . . . ?'

'Because you will write about it. And then we shall see what happens.'

'But what are you hoping to achieve?'

'The Harrises were friends of mine. I'd like the police to re-open the case.'

They walked to the car. He paused and said, 'Do you know of the Hungarian writer Lajos Zilahy?' She shook her head. 'Many years ago he wrote a three-page short story about an old carpenter who died in Budapest. As his friends and relations died off one by one there was eventually no one anywhere who remembered him. Therefore he ceased to exist and disappeared from the earth.' He smiled at her. 'The name of the story was "But For This . . . "'

Alex paid the garage for changing her wheel and was at the car loading her camera with the new film when Georges Corton stopped in the Mercedes.

'I hear you had a flat tyre,' he said. 'You should not leave your car here.'

'Do you think someone will harm it?' she said sarcastically.

'Not at all, but sometimes the rock chips from the blasting fly this way. It might get scratched.'

'But I can't get to your house.' She pointed to the rockfall.

'Please follow me.' Then he smiled. 'We hope you will take luncheon with us.'

He took a track that wound round the back of Carriac and soon they reached his house on the far side of the village. She parked under a walnut tree.

They ate outside on the terrace. It was a simple meal of pâté, a cheese soufflé and fruit. Georges opened a bottle of Chablis, making a performance out of tasting it and filling glasses.

'It's not the finest,' he said, rolling it about his tongue and making a faint snorting noise through his nose. 'But it comes from the vineyard of Montmains so it is not without pedigree.'

The Cortons went out of their way to be charming. Inevitably the talk returned to the subject of the village and once again they were at pains to stress its links with Britain.

As she spoke Mary kept flicking her eyes to Neville as though waiting for a comment that never came. Alex realised that the lunch was as much for his benefit as hers.

Then, before she could ask any questions, the topic was steered away from the village. She found herself listening to Georges talking about the need for France to be ruled again by a king.

'Two hundred years ago we chopped off the head of our king and we've regretted it ever since. You only have to look at our newspapers when your Prince Charles and Princess Diana come to France. Even *Le Monde* reports every time they glance at each other; what she wears; what they eat and drink; if there is a smudge under her eyes; if her hair is done a little differently. They are surrogates for the real thing.'

Alex saw Mary look away and switch her mind into neutral as though she had heard this many times before.

'We turned de Gaulle into a king,' Georges was saying. 'We turned Bonaparte into a king. We are an ancient people and we *need* a king.'

He paused to take a mouthful of wine and Mary hastily intervened and said to Alex, 'Is someone here looking after you, I mean from the *syndicat d'initiative*?'

Before she could reply, Georges said, 'Max Wellmann is looking after her. Not so?'

Alex saw a look dart between husband and wife.

'I had a flat tyre and he was kind enough to take me into Sarlat this morning.'

'Be careful of Wellmann, he's a communist,' Georges said.

'Don't exaggerate.' Mary turned to Alex. 'Anyone who isn't a royalist is a communist in Georges' opinion.'

'I found him very helpful.'

'Did he show you his caves?' Mary said.

'He spends hours scratching about looking for cave paintings and bones,' Georges said. 'He hasn't anything better to do with his time.'

'He took me down to see—' Halfway through the sentence Alex realised she did not want to mention the Harrises, nor Max's suspicions. '—to the river to show me the view. We passed a little cottage. He said it was where the hunchback—'

'Petit Louis.'

'Yes, where Petit Louis had lived.'

Neville had been eating a pear and now his knife dropped with a clang on to the plate. He swung his chair away from the table and began to wheel it swiftly along the terrace. Mary followed him.

'Have I said something wrong?' Alex asked.

Georges was looking down the terrace towards his wife and step-son and did not reply.

After lunch Alex walked to the PTT and phoned David's private office number.

'David Clarke.'

'It's me.'

'How are things?'

His voice sounded preoccupied.

'Can you talk?'

'Not really.'

'Oh, I was just phoning to say have a lovely holiday. You leave tomorrow, don't you?'

'That's kind of you. Thank you.'

'Well . . . '

'Let me call you back.'

She didn't know the Cortons' number and she did not want to wait at the post office.

'It's not possible. Give Simon my love. 'Bye.'

She put down the receiver feeling frustrated and angry. Then she went to her room and typed up her notes. About mid-afternoon she decided to go to the Harris house and photograph it. The clouds had come up and a breeze was rustling the leaves of the poplar trees along the river. She took some time to find the right road and only realised she was on it when she saw the hunchback's cottage.

9

The burnt-out house had a different feel to it as she got out of her car. The clouds had darkened and the air had become chilly. There was a feel of rain. She stood for a moment, noticing for the first time the scraps of paper blowing in the breeze, the roses engulfed by grass, the weeds growing up in the middle of the gravel drive. And over it all was the smell of old burning.

Photographing the house was a backstop. She might need it, she might not. But she would definitely need the hunchback's house, for Petit Louis was very much part of her story about Neville.

His cottage lay north of the Harris place and she was about to get back into the car and drive to it when she noticed a path leading in that direction. Picking up her camera bag, she pushed through a thicket of wild bamboo and found herself looking at the rear of the cottage.

It was single-storeyed with a tiled roof. Once the walls had been whitewashed but they were now a dirty grey.

A pile of cordwood was stacked, waiting to be cut up by a circular saw which was attached by a belt to an old tractor. There was a chicken-house and run without any chickens, a wooden shed, an old broken barn, a car so derelict she could not tell what make it had been, an upturned rusty wheelbarrow – and a lorry.

It was an old flatbed lorry with raised sides, which had been used, she imagined, for delivering the firewood which Petit Louis had sold for a living. She took several wide-angled shots and then used the zoom to bring up the cottage itself. In doing so she saw, through the telephoto, that the back door was fastened by a padlock which seemed not to have been properly snapped shut.

She was tempted to get some shots of the interior. She looked around but the place was as silent as the grave. Quickly she moved to the doorway, slipped the padlock from the hasp and pushed the door.

The interior was dark. All the windows had been covered by newspaper but there was a light switch at the door and she turned on the single bulb hanging in the middle of the room.

There were only two rooms, with an archway separating them. The one she had entered was the living quarters with an old gas cooker, a table, two chairs, a crazed porcelain sink with wooden draining board, and a sideboard. Everything was a shambles. Drawers in the sideboard had been emptied on to the floor, pictures had been taken from nails on the wall and smashed.

The cooking equipment had been pulled from a cupboard under the sink. There was broken crockery and glass everywhere.

She moved, crunching on the glass, to what had been the bedroom. The bed was unmade. Blankets had been dropped on the floor and the mattress had been partly cut open, allowing some horsehair to spill out. Drawers from a chest had been pulled out and clothing lay in a heap.

She wondered who had vandalised the place. Kids? And what had they been looking for? Was Petit Louis one of those hoarders suspected of having a fortune under his bed?

She checked the flash and raised the camera to her eye. Just then she heard the soft thump . . . thump . . . thump . . . of a large-engined motorcycle. She put her eye to a tear in the newspaper at one of the front windows. A man was standing some distance up the lane, watching the cottage.

Quickly she made for the back door, switched off the light and let herself quietly out. Then she realised that he would have a view of the path back to the burnt-out house and she did not want to be seen.

She ran silently to the other side of the lorry. At that moment the motorcyclist walked round the side of the house. There was something frightening about the stealth with which he approached the building. It was as though he knew there was someone inside – no, not someone, Alex – and was coming for her.

She had not had time to replace the padlock but had pulled the door closed. Now, very gently, he pushed it open and went in.

She waited for a few moments to make sure there was no one else following him, then she rose from her crouching position at the side of the lorry and was about to run the few yards to the fringing tangle of bush, when he came out of the house.

She froze. He looked around quickly and then went to the old shed. He stuck his head inside, came out, and went over to the woodpile.

She desperately wanted to make a run for her car in the Harris drive but he was between her and the path.

He made for the poultry house and went round the back. Silently she opened the door of the lorry's cab and crawled into it, pulling the door to behind her. She lay on the floor and then raised her head to the level of the windscreen. He was on the path, looking into the clumps of willow and bamboo.

The inside of the cab smelled of sweat, caporal tobacco and diesel. On the floor beside her was a battered vacuum flask, a tin lunchbox and a large torch.

She looked up just in time to see the man cross to the house and re-enter it. She opened the door of the lorry and, grabbing the torch as a weapon, ran to the woodpile. She managed to keep this between her and the cottage, while she raced for the path.

Bamboos lashed at her, branches caught at her clothes and hair. She ran as hard as she could. She flung herself into her car, started the engine, and drove out of the gate in a flurry of gravel. She put down her foot and passed the cottage at speed. The motorcycle had been pushed off the road and was partly hidden in the trees. She had only a fleeting glimpse and then she was past it and gone.

She drove fast all the way back to Carriac, her eyes flicking constantly to the rearview mirror, but no black figure astride a motorcycle came into view. She was rattled and shaky, and only felt safe once she was back in her bedroom with the door locked.

Had he been following her at the cottage, or was it just her imagination? Had he been following *anyone*? He might have come to the cottage for reasons entirely unconnected with her. Perhaps he was a relative of Petit Louis. Perhaps he had inherited the place. But something inside her refused to accept so convenient a scenario.

He seemed to know the house. She brought up in her mind the picture of him looking behind the woodpile and in the shed. He had been looking for some*one* and not some*thing*.

She kicked off her shoes, lay down on the bed and stared up at the ceiling. She felt exposed, a stranger in a foreign land, with every hand against her. But come,

come! No self-pity. And anyway, all hands weren't against her. Mary Corton and her husband had been pleasant and Max Wellmann warm and friendly.

Yet it was Max who had made her see below the surface of whatever was happening in Carriac – if indeed anything was happening at all. Now she wished he hadn't.

But most of all she wished that David was there. If he had come as she'd first suggested she would have been able to transfer her apprehensions and uneasiness. Rightly or wrongly she always felt secure when he was around. Security was a dull word, yet dullness was the last adjective she would have applied to David. She had a feeling that in the final analysis he would be able to cope with most situations.

She had first met him when she was preparing an article on publishing for a national newspaper. He had not been with Byrom & Lancing for more than a couple of years. He had been spoken of as a whizz-kid and had been hired to take the firm out of the doldrums and into the front line.

It was the first warm day of early spring and she had taken him to a Lebanese restaurant in Bayswater. The meal had been polite and formal. At first he had been reserved but then, on the second bottle of wine, had begun to thaw. He had started to gossip and tell her stories that could have landed both of them in court if she had used them. Instead she put her notebook away, sat back, and allowed herself to be amused.

They sat on until well after three o'clock and then he said he was going to walk back to the office through the park. She had walked with him. Then they had found themselves strolling away from his office in the brilliant sunlight. They had gone to Kensington Gardens, past the statue of Speke and on to the pond and watched small boys sail boats. He told her about Simon and about Susan and the cerebral haemorrhage that had killed her.

They went on walking all the way round by the Albert Memorial and back along the Serpentine to the Peter Pan statue.

'What are you going to do now?' he said.

'Go home, I suppose.'

'I've enjoyed this.'

'So have I.'

'Have dinner with me?'

She paused.

'Look, I've got to go home and see to Simon. Come with me. We'll show you how the other half lives.'

She smiled. 'I'd love to.'

He had driven her out to Twickenham and she had met Simon. 'This is my new friend, Alexandra,' David had said.

'Everyone calls me Alex.'

Simon had swung his intense dark eyes on her. He was judging her as he judged all his father's women, she guessed, against the yardstick of his mother.

The exterior of the house was ordinary in a street of ordinary houses, but the inside was bright and cheerful, with yellow and orange curtains and chair covers. The kitchen was panelled in pine. The furniture was comfortable and had once been expensive. The house gave a sense of being loved and lived in and she felt instantly at home.

David had called a baby-sitter who lived nearby, a teenage girl called Sally, who seemed to know the house as well as its owners. It was all friendly and neighbourly and to Alex, who missed her own family, it seemed infinitely desirable.

They dined in Richmond and returned to the house

about ten and found Simon and Sally playing Scrabble. They joined in as kibitzers and immediately the room became loud with argument. Alex was struck by Simon's knowledge.

By eleven o'clock Simon was in bed, Sally had gone and she and David were sitting downstairs having a last glass of wine and listening to the first act of *Norma*.

She began to experience that sense of unease at what was being planned in David's mind and she became even more uneasy when he rose and came to sit on the arm of her chair. He reached for her hand, held it and said, 'I'd like to see you again.'

'When?'

'Will you have lunch with me tomorrow?'

That's how it had begun.

10

There was a knock on Alex's door and she let in Mary Corton.

'I'm sorry to disturb you,' Mary said. 'But there's something I want to discuss.' She went to the window and stood looking out for a moment. 'I don't quite know how to put this so I'll say it without any frills. When Georges told me you were coming here I wasn't pleased.'

'Because of Neville?'

'Exactly. Then, when I began thinking about it, I wondered whether your presence might not help.'

'How?'

'I'd like you to talk to him. Not with Georges or me there, just the two of you. Something you might say, some inflection in your voice, anything, might trigger off a reaction.'

What could she say? Alex thought. It was like being asked to sing a much-loved song to someone in a coma. If she were Mary she would be begging, too.

'When?'

'Now would be a good time. There's nothing much on TV.'

Alex followed her to Neville's room. He was sitting in his usual place with his back to the room, facing the window, and she saw the electronic game on his knees.

'I've brought you a visitor,' Mary said, pulling up a chair for her. He swung his face slowly in their direction as though it was a radar dish. Then, with forced bonhomie, she said, 'I'm going to leave you two to have a nice chat.' She went out of the room and closed the door.

'I'd like to try and help you, Neville,' Alex said. 'What would you like to talk about? Normally I'd ask you to tell me about yourself, that's always a good way to get started. I've used it a lot in my job. But of course you can't tell me. So let's turn it around and I'll tell you about me.'

He was not prepossessing. He was large and puffy and his hair fell over the collar of his shirt, but not in a fashionable way.

She spoke about her early life, about her mother who lived near the south coast and about her father, an architect, who had died a few years before. She spoke about her tennis and going to university.

Neville switched on the screen. Plink-plonk . . . plink-plonk . . . the manikins went round and round and his fingers darted to press the right buttons at the right micro-second.

It was like someone turning his back on her at a cocktail party and she felt a stab of irritation. Remorselessly she went on through her university career and then into journalism. She told him about some of the places she had been and stories she had written, but he appeared to have no interest.

Plink-plonk . . . Plink-plonk.

'That's why I've come to Carriac.' she said. 'To write a story about the tragedy. Not the kind of story other journalists have written, but the story within the story.'

She'd been looking down at the screen on his lap

as she spoke and saw a manikin tumble into a river. Neville had been too slow on the buttons.

'There *is* a story within the story,' she said. 'I'm beginning to see its outline. I met Dr Wellmann. He told me there had been another tragedy. A couple called Harris. But you'd know about them, of course.'

The manikins tumbled into the river one after the other. Plink... plink... plink... He suddenly switched it off.

'He took me to see the house. It's sad seeing a burnt house. I took some pictures. He showed me where the hunchback lived.'

Neville's fingers laced into each other like small white snakes.

'Your mother's very proud of you. You're part of my story too, Neville, because you're a hero. Not many people would have done what you did. Dr Wellmann says you lay there for hours and that any sudden movement would have brought the rocks down on top of you.'

His face had grown rigid.

'I wonder if I should talk about it? Your mother didn't tell me not to. I wonder if this is what everyone's been avoiding. I mean, talking to you about what actually happened. Dr Wellmann said you've become trapped within yourself.

'If I were able to get the story from you the way I want to write it I would want to ask you how you got there, what you were doing when the cliff fell.

'Years ago I read a book called *The Bridge of San Louis Rey*. It's about a bridge that collapsed in South America and about the people who were on the bridge when it fell. It tells how they got there and who they were and why they were there at that particular moment. That's how I'd like to do this story. I'd like to know why Petit

Louis was there. And who he was. I've been to his cottage . . . '

His eyes were burning at her now.

'I took some photographs there, too. He'll be part of my story: the tragedy of a small hunchback in the wrong place at the wrong time. But I've got to find out more about him. Who he was and why he was there.

'You see, Neville, what I mean by a story within a story? It's like a play within a play.'

His face had turned to stone. Even the eyes were unblinking. Then she saw two tears squeeze themselves from the corner of those wide-open eyes and run silently down the sides of his nose.

When Alex reached the restaurant that evening the terrace was empty. She took a table under one of the lights and wished she had brought a book to read. But what she wished most was that this was an English pub where she could order a ham sandwich.

She didn't feel like eating but she was hungry. She knew that if she did not eat now there were no snack bars, no pubs, no all-night supermarkets or delis, nowhere she could go and buy a packet of biscuits or a slab of chocolate. She glanced at the menu. Soup, trout, *contrefilet* and *frites*, crême caramel.

She felt wound up like a violin string. The man searching the cottage was still vivid in her mind.

Where had he come from? Had he seen her at the Harris house? And why had he come?

Abruptly she rose, went to the telephone in the small reception and phoned David in London.

'Hello,' a thin voice said.

'Hello Simon, it's Alex.'

Silence.

'Is your father there?'

'No.'

She glanced at her watch. He should be home. 'Isn't he back from work?'

'Yes.'

She could visualise Simon standing by the wall telephone in the pine-panelled kitchen, perhaps with the TV on, impatient to go back to it.

'Can you tell me how long he'll be?'

'He went out to buy some cigarettes.'

'Oh, then he won't be long. Would you ask him to ring this number when he comes back? Have you got a pencil?'

He took it down and then said, 'Goodbye,' and she heard the line go dead.

She went back to her table and the elderly grey-haired woman of the day before took her order. She seemed no friendlier.

The image of Neville's dead white face with the two droplets coursing down the sides of his nose, rose in her mind.

She had felt like leaving the Corton house then. Not because she was afraid but because she felt she was getting into something she did not understand. Normally she was cool and objective about her stories but now she seemed about to become part of the story herself. And what she desperately did not want was to become the story within the story.

Just then the phone rang and before the old woman could reach it Alex ran across the terrace and lifted the receiver.

'Hi,' David said.

'God, I'm so glad to hear your voice!'

'Sorry I couldn't talk earlier today but I had Whittaker in my room.' Whittaker was the chairman of Byrom & Lancing.

'It doesn't matter now.'

'You sound strained.'

'I don't mean to. Well, yes, I suppose I am a bit.'

She told him as briefly as she could what had happened since she arrived, trying not to make too much of a drama out of it.

'It sounds like "Bad Day at Black Rock",' he said. 'Stranger comes to village and finds the natives hostile. Let me get this straight. You say this Dr Wellmann thinks the English couple was murdered?'

'Yes.'

'But they've got nothing to do with the main tragedy?'

'No, the house was burnt some months ago.'

'Do you know anything about Wellmann? You sound as though you trust him.'

'I do. He's friendly and warm.'

'You don't think he's having you on?'

'What would be the point?'

'But you *were* followed this afternoon?'

'Yes, I'm pretty sure of that.'

'Look, it's obvious that the last thing the village wants is a journalist snooping about and writing yet another story about the tragedy. Don't forget these people make their living out of tourists.'

'I suppose so.'

'You couldn't . . . I mean, you haven't got enough material to leave and come and join us?'

'No. Not yet. I can't let Robin Akers down. He's saving space. Oh hell, don't pay any attention to me. I'm just feeling homesick, wishing I was back in London. I haven't felt this way since I was a child.'

'I know the feeling.'

'Anyway, have a lovely holiday. You must be all packed up.'

'Yes, we are.'

'I wish I was going to be with you.'
'I wish so too. What's the weather like down there?'
'Warm. I'll probably swim tomorrow.'
'It's bloody awful here. And in Brittany, too. We've got a gale and rain. Just the sort of weather for playing on beaches.'
'I'd better go,' she said.

The village was dark and silent as she walked back to the Cortons' house. She picked her way along the path through the rubble, past van der Meulen's wheelbarrow. She heard a sound, as though someone had scraped a shoe on a rock, up near the cliff. She paused, looking up into the darkness, feeling afraid, and wondering if she should go back to the hotel. But she was halfway to the Cortons' house now. She went on, hurrying, trying not to run.

Everything she had once thought about Carriac, all the sun-filled holidays, the picnics on the little *plage*, the meals with her father and mother and brother at the Bellevue, many of her best childhood memories, had been erased by this brooding and sinister place. She wanted to leave as soon as she could, but there was at least a week's work ahead of her.

From the drive she looked up at the house and saw the green phosphorescence in Neville's room. She went in the front door and heard Mary in the kitchen. She was stacking the dishwasher. They talked for ten minutes and Alex began to feel better. She said goodnight and turned along the hall to the bottom of the staircase. The lights were dim. She heard a noise behind her. For a dreadful second she thought she was going to feel a hand at her neck. Then a voice said, 'Miss Bridgman.'

Georges was standing in his study door. 'Won't you come in for a moment?'

As she entered the study she thought it was like a room in a Scottish castle, a place where ancient battles were still fought out in memory and the tools of war revered.

She had glimpses of swords and lances, flags and pennants, armour and books, then Georges indicated a chair. He sat at his desk, the top of which was lit by a shell lamp. Behind him she could see an orange pennant with forked tongue and below it some words stencilled on to the wall which she could not make out in the deep shadows.

'My wife told me what she asked you to do,' Georges said. 'It was very good of you.'

'I would like to help. But I'm afraid I didn't achieve much.'

'Who can tell? Something might have penetrated his mind. You can see how helpless we are.'

'Wouldn't he react better to those two young men? I mean, they're his friends.'

'Of course. I've asked them several times but . . . the young can be very cruel, Miss Bridgman. Anyway, how have you been getting on with your researches?'

'I'm anathema in the village,' she said. 'It's going to be hard work.'

'Most of them are peasants, or were before the tourists began to come. Peasants are always suspicious.'

It was the voice of Sire de Corton, she thought, remembering what Max Wellmann had told her. She was surprised he had not described them as villeins. 'We will be only too pleased to help where we can.'

Grabbing the opportunity, she said, 'I've been wondering about Petit Louis. Neville's story is important for any article written about that night and afterwards.'

'What were you wondering?'

'Why Petit Louis was there. He sold wood, didn't he?'

'Correct.'

'The cliff collapsed about midnight. He wouldn't be delivering at that time. And his cottage is about six kilometres away.'

'You know where he lives?'

'I've been there. Dr Wellmann took me,' she reminded him. 'And he also took me to the Harris house.'

'I wonder why he did that?'

'He wanted to show me that the rockfall was not the first accident.' She emphasised the word.

'But as far as I know Max doesn't think the fire was an accident,' Georges said.

'No.'

'Everything is a conspiracy to Max. That's how communists think.' He leaned back and his face was lost in shadow. All she could see clearly were his plump hands in the circlet of light. 'You see he has no past and people who have no past have no future. This is our past.' He indicated the room. 'Wellmann has nothing of this.'

'Don't you think it's dangerous to live in the past?'

'My dear Miss Bridgman, it was Thucydides who said that history came in cycles. The present cycle is declining, the past will reassert itself.'

'Do you really think the past was better than the present?'

'What is "better"? Nobler certainly.'

After a few more minutes in which he described the attractions of the fourteenth century, she rose and excused herself. He followed her to the door of his study. 'I want you to tell me if he speaks, you understand? Not my wife. Not anyone else. Me.' He was speaking softly but there was a sudden hint of menace in his voice.

She went up to her room and locked the door once more. Before putting on the bathroom light she went in and looked at Neville's windows. In spite of the fact that the night was cool, they were open. She heard the thud . . . thud . . . of rock music.

She wrote up her notes and went to bed, trying to erase the memory of the man at the cottage. She tried to think of David. He'd be asleep now in his house in London. What was she going to do about him? Let things drift on as they were? The trouble was, she did not know what she could do to change them, short of marrying him and taking on instant motherhood.

A little after two in the morning she woke suddenly. She heard a noise and feared that someone was in the room. There was a half-moon sending its light through the branches of a tree; the chair seemed to crouch, the wardrobe was like a square black hole into another world. She switched on the light. The room was as she had last seen it, perfectly peaceful, the suitcase, her clothes and cameras, all undisturbed. The door to the bathroom was open and she could see that it, too, was empty.

Had the noise come from the garden? She went to the window but could see little, for it was a shadowy place of shrubs and trees. Then she remembered the hunchback's torch.

She scooped it up from the chair and flicked it on. Nothing happened. The batteries were dead. She got back into bed, put the light on again and looked at the torch. She could do with one, she thought, if her nights were going to be disturbed. It was a big torch and would give a good beam but it felt unnaturally light. She unscrewed the end. There were no batteries at all. Instead, as she turned it vertically, a piece of paper fell out.

It was a photographic receipt for processing three rolls of Kodachrome 64 in the name of Louis Seurel.

11

'Look at this,' Max Wellman said. 'You can see where the outline of the house was.'

Alex had climbed up the rubble-strewn slope that had once been three rows of houses and had joined him at the base of the cliff. She could look down over the area that had been devastated, to the river where van der Meulen was emptying a load of stones. Above her she could hear the whining and clattering of the cranes at the top of the cliffs, and below a bulldozer was moving the rubble off the road. It was soon to reopen to single-line traffic. The outline of a gable was clearly marked on the cliff-face.

'A whole row of houses was built up against the rock,' Max said. 'They would have been the first houses in the village so the rock here has been covered by stone walls and mortar for centuries.'

There were other houses whose rear walls abutted on the cliff but several of them had not been demolished cleanly and would have to wait for labourers to take them to pieces rock by rock.

'No one knows what lies behind them or what's been covered up all these years,' he said. He was wearing his long khaki dust-coat and a floppy white hat. The morning sun was strong.

'This whole area is full of strange historical curiosities.

Who'd have thought that rhinoceros and bison once lived here? They've found bones in caves under Domme.'

He pointed to large cavities in the cliff-face fifteen metres above the ground. 'That's where the peasants took refuge from your English soldiers in the Hundred Years' War. Even before that they would climb up there on ladders and pull them up after them to escape the knights who came back this way from the Holy Land.'

He sat down on a piece of rock and fanned his broad, scarred face. 'Are you interested in all this background for your article?'

'Of course. It's just what I need. I've been here a dozen times before and I never knew the story.'

'This was Aquitaine. England held it for three hundred years. You'll even find that some of the French families have English names. There's a baker in Carlux called Bailey and a watchmaker in Souillac called Williams. And I've seen tombstones and parish records with names like Portman and Abel, even Rhodes.'

'I wonder how Georges Corton relates that to history?'

'Why?'

She told him briefly about her conversation with Georges the night before.

Max smiled. 'If it wasn't so uncomfortable Georges would walk around in armour. He's infected those young men, too. Derek Blackwood's more French than the French. You've seen his car and the way he dresses?'

She nodded. 'That's all because of Georges.'

'It's given him a certain style, I suppose.'

'He used to be a nice kid. So were Neville and Pierre, but all this historical nationalism changed them. Most young men in this country are arrogant. These three have become impossibly so.'

'He calls you a communist,' Alex said, trying for a reaction.

Max laughed. 'To Georges anyone who is anti-capital punishment and who doesn't go to church is a communist. Come and have some coffee.'

They sat on the hotel terrace in the hot sunshine.

'I went back to the Harris house,' she said.

'Oh?' The expression in the blue eyes became quizzical.

She told him about her visit to the house and to Petit Louis' cottage.

He frowned when she mentioned the motorcyclist. 'I only know of one person who dresses like that – Pierre Chervas. But what would he want at Petit Louis' place?'

'Perhaps he'd gone to the Harris house and followed me from there?'

'Why was he there? I don't think he knew them. Even if he did, the fire happened months ago. No, it has to be something else, something different.'

'Or new?'

'What?'

'Me?' She said it lightly but the expression on his face chilled her.

The Citroën nosed slowly into the Harris drive and came to a halt. Derek Blackwood and Pierre Chervas got out. Derek was dressed in his white suit with black trilby and grey snakeskin shoes.

'Show me,' he said.

Chervas, dressed more informally in jeans and a T-shirt, took him towards the house.

'The car was parked here. She took pictures from over there and from the far side and then came through here.'

They entered by what had once been the front door. Blackwood stepped fastidiously over charred beams. He placed a cigarette in his onyx holder and lit it. 'And here?'

'Yes, here too. But why?'

'How many?'

'Six, seven. I mean, why photograph a burnt house?'

Derek looked at him with distaste. 'You know, sometimes I want to cry for you, you're so fucking dumb.'

Pierre turned to look at him. He was much bigger than Derek yet in some indefinable way seemed the less strong of the two. 'What have I said now?' His big, low-browed face was showing his hurt feelings.

'The question isn't why she took the pictures, not the first question anyway. The first question is how the hell did she know about the place? It's off the road. Why come here?'

'Maybe she was going down to the river.'

'And maybe she wasn't. Who wanted the fire investigated again?'

'Dr Max.'

'Brilliant.'

'Where did they go after leaving Sarlat? When you didn't follow them?'

'*Here?* But what for?'

'Jesus, she's a journalist. It's copy.'

He picked his way out of the house and went along the path to Petit Louis' cottage.

'You're sure she went inside?' he said.

'Pretty sure. The padlock wasn't as I'd left it.'

Derek walked slowly round the building.

'How long was she inside?'

'Couldn't have been more than a minute.'

'Then she couldn't have found anything.'

They went inside.

'What difference would it make? She wouldn't know what she'd found anyway.'

'It depends on what Dr Max told her. She's not stupid. Come on, let's have another try.'

'What? Again?'

'Again.'

'But we spent hours—'

'That was before she came along.'

They began to cut up the mattress in the small bedroom, separating the old coir in their fingers as they searched. After a while they went outside and began to search the truck.

'There's one more question about your childhood,' Alex said to Mary. 'When did you first want to be a writer? Was it after you'd left school?'

'I think it was while I was still at school. I could always write essays – compositions we used to call them in those days. I loved writing them.'

They were in the tower room, Mary at her desk, Alex in one of the two easy chairs with rounded backs made to fit against the walls.

Alex flipped back a few pages to check if there were any earlier questions she had not dealt with and then said, 'Can you tell me what happened that night? I mean, from your personal observations.'

'I didn't have any. Not at the beginning anyway. I've always slept badly so I usually take a pill. I didn't hear a thing when it happened though people said it sounded like the river coming down in flood. Max came with the news.'

'And Monsieur Corton? Was he already there?'

'No, he'd been at a Lodge meeting in Souillac. He's a Mason. Several people around here are members of the same Lodge. He was on his way home. He got there a few minutes after it happened.'

'And found Neville?'

'Not at first. It was pitch dark. You couldn't see your hand in front of your face.'

Alex took her words down, quoting her directly.

'The problem was . . . ' She hesitated. 'You see, Neville had been with Derek and Pierre that night. They'd been to a disco in Sarlat in Derek's car and he had dropped Neville off in the village. He was walking home when it happened.'

The interview went on for more than an hour, then Alex said, 'Dr Wellmann told me that your husband is an expert on the Middle Ages.'

'He's got every book you've ever heard of. He probably knows more about chivalry than the experts. He should have lived then – or so he keeps telling me.'

'Was Neville interested?'

'Yes he was. And it brought them together in a way. You see Neville's father . . . well, that's another story . . . but after we were divorced Neville was jealous and suspicious of my men friends. Then along came Georges. Neville was dead set against us marrying. In fact he used to get a high temperature every time we went out together. So it wasn't easy at first.

'After we were married and came down here things got better. Neville was about eight and he met Pierre and Derek. It was then that Georges began to go back into his family history. It gave him an interest, I suppose. And it infected the boys like magic. They became hooked on heraldry and knightly tales and Georges used to read them stories from his books and tell them about wars and battles and then they used to go out and re-enact them.

'They'd dress up and put on masques on the lawn

or in the garage if the weather was bad. Derek was the leader. He began to collect armour and swords, anything to do with chivalry. I'm told he has a better collection than Georges now.'

'And Neville? Does he have a collection?'

'He's got a cupboard full of things. It's supposed to be his secret cupboard.' She smiled. 'No one's allowed to go near it. He's the only one with a key.'

'What sort of things? Swords?'

'I suppose so. Though what he would do with a sword I can't imagine. He wouldn't hurt a fly. He's not that sort of person.'

'What sort of person is he, Mrs Corton?'

Mary looked thoughtful for a few moments and then said, 'To tell you the truth, and I wouldn't want this quoted of course, I've never been quite sure. He's an introvert, I suppose. But I've never been quite certain of what was going on in his head. He went to boarding school in England and all his reports said he was a loner. That's why I've always been pleased he had Derek and Pierre, even if they were a bit wild.'

'Their families are wealthy, aren't they?'

'Pots of money. And the boys have always had large allowances. Pierre's smashed up I don't know how many motorcycles and Derek's had that Citroën of his rebuilt from scratch. It must have cost a fortune.'

'Does Neville have a car?'

'Oh, yes, you can't really live here without one. Brand new Peugeot sports coupé. He's only had it a few weeks.'

'One day he'll drive it again,' Alex said sympathetically. Then, 'He's got marvellous hands.'

'What do you mean?'

'Co-ordination. He's so quick with his game. It made me wonder—'

'About what?'

'Why he never writes. I know he can't talk but he could write.'

'We've given him a dozen kinds of pads and a dozen pens. We even gave him a word processor. But he's never written a single word.'

12

Plink-plonk . . . plink-plonk . . .
Round and round went the manikins.
They had names. Splendid names. Sire Geoffroy de Charny, Sire Baudouin d'Annequin and, Neville himself, the Count of Dammartin . . .
He had wanted to be de Charny and so had Pierre when they had first heard about him. He would have been eight years old then and his step-father, Georges, had been telling the three of them about chivalry and knighthood one wet winter afternoon.
But Derek had grabbed de Charny just as he grabbed most things he wanted.
It wasn't that he was physically stronger than Neville or Pierre, just the opposite in fact. Pierre was the biggest and the most powerful and even Neville, who had outgrown his strength at school and been called 'beanpole', was bigger and more rugged.
But Derek had something inside him that was more potent than muscle. Neville had always been afraid of Derek and he knew that these feelings were duplicated by Pierre.
They had played at being knights while other kids played football. If Georges had not been so much a fourteenth-century person himself the craze might have lasted a week or so. But he was there to teach, to encourage, to inspire. And around the walls and in

the cupboards of his room were banners and swords, helms and greaves, breastplates and daggers, lances and battle-axes.

They were allowed to look and touch and even use them in their games and masques. What might have been a world of the imagination only, was there in reality.

To Georges the Age of Chivalry was highlighted by nobility and always he came back to the Battle of Poitiers in 1356, one of the key battles of the Hundred Years' War between France and England. Neville could almost hear him now as he spoke of the moment when, the battle already lost to the English, the French king took his knights into the thick of the fighting.

'But first they dismounted and took off their spurs and cut off the long-pointed toes of their poulaines. Then they shortened their lances to make them more efficient for stabbing.

'The oriflamme was awarded to Geoffroy de Charny to carry, because he was known as the perfect knight.

'Then the king said, "You have cursed the English and have longed to measure swords with them. Remember the wrongs they have done to France." And with that they gave the battle cry and rode into the mêlée.'

De Charny was killed and that made him all the more romantic. D'Annequin and Dammartin were taken prisoner.

'It was a defeat for France,' Georges said, 'but a victory for nobility.'

For a long time Neville had felt tears come to his eyes when he thought of de Charny carrying the banner of France to his death. He had wanted to *be* de Charny – but couldn't while Derek was. In fact, he knew he was lucky to be a French knight at all, being English bred and therefore of the enemy. It was only because

Georges was French and because of his collection that Neville was accepted. Derek was only half French but no one mentioned that.

Over the years the three had never lost their feeling for knightly ways. But it was only in the last few years that Derek had begun to change his rôle from sentimental pretence to active involvement.

'You don't think it was all chivalry and courtly love, do you?' he said. 'That's just Georges' talk. God no! They were men! They took what society owed them! They became a political force! They *changed* society!'

Taking what society owed them meant shoplifting in Sarlat. Becoming a political force meant attending National Front meetings when le Pen was making a speech. Changing society meant beating up a young left-winger in Souillac one night.

It had been exciting. The Knights of the Oriflamme, they had called themselves. He had given little thought to what they were doing, what road they were taking.

This was the end of that road; this room, this wheel-chair, these little figures that went round and round . . . plink-plonk . . . plink-plonk . . .

'She interviewed me today,' Mary said.

Max Wellmann was stretched out in one of the easy chairs in her tower study.

'Difficult?'

'No. She was easy. She's interested in Petit Louis.'

'I showed her his house. It's only natural. I mean she will be writing about Neville.'

'Georges doesn't like her.'

'Why?'

'Maybe because she's not impressed by him.'

'He's old enough to be her father.'

'That's never worried Georges before.'

'Where is he, by the way?'

'At a Lodge meeting. The journalist is eating at the hotel.'

He frowned. 'One day all this will be over. Things will return to normal.'

'It was hardly normal before.'

'It was the best we could do.'

She decided to change the subject. 'How is Thomas?'

'The same. He hasn't stopped digging. You know, I always thought he was wrong marrying Marie. Middle-age in pursuit of youth is always somewhat pathetic.'

'She was marvellous to him! I mean he wasn't everyone's cup of tea. I always thought Thomas came right out of the Old Testament.'

He shrugged. 'At least he's got something to occupy himself. I'm worried about what will happen to him when he comes to the end and finds . . . well, nothing.'

'In a way he's like Neville,' she said. 'Both ruined by the same thing.'

'Neville's younger. He's got more chance of coming out of it.'

'You really think it's trauma?'

'Positive.'

'I haven't prayed for years but now I find myself doing it two and three times a day.'

'It won't go on for ever. I promise you that. One day he'll come out of it, as though it was a dream.'

'Do you think he suspects?'

'No. But you're in a better position to know. Do you?'

'Sometimes I wonder.'

He took out his cigar case.

'I wouldn't,' she said. 'The smell lingers.'

'Of course.' He put it away.

'You took her to the Harris house, she says.'

'I wanted to give her something to dig into. I want to know what she's uncovering.'

'You sound like Georges.'

'You never know what she might stumble on. *She* won't understand, she might not even recognise she has stumbled on anything.'

'What have you told her?'

'Just the usual.'

'I asked her to talk to Neville today.'

'Why?'

'In case she said something that would break the silence.'

He nodded. 'That's good. But nothing?'

'Nothing.'

'What did she talk about?'

Mary reached across her desk and switched on a small hand tape recorder. There was a hiss of blank tape then a metallic voice saying, 'I'd like to try and help you, Neville . . . '

They listened in silence until the end, then they looked at each other. After a pause Max said, 'The play within the play. A story within a story. She put it well. I hope she does not become a central character. It could be dangerous.'

Alex parked her car at the end of the lane which led to Derek Blackwood's mill-house. The rain of the previous day had formed puddles in the car tracks and she picked her way along the grassy side.

She had telephoned Derek earlier that day when she was trying, and failing, to set up interviews with some of the villagers. She knew she would have to speak to him some time but she had been subconsciously putting off the meeting.

She wasn't sure why, only that she felt an unease at the thought of being alone with him. So she had asked him to meet her for a drink at the Bellevue. Instead he had, surprisingly, pressed her to lunch with him. She could not find an excuse and so, telling herself that she might get some good copy from his life-style, she crossed the river.

As she moved deeper down the lane she lost sight of her own car and of the road. The growth was prodigious. Grass came up to her calves, brambles and blackberry vines formed impenetrable barriers on either side. When she saw the Citroën, glowing in the noon sun, she felt a sense of relief. Much of it, she realised, was caused by the fact that Pierre Chervas' motorcycle was not there too. She could not be certain that it was he who had followed her to Petit Louis' cottage – for that matter she could not be sure she *had* been followed – but she was glad anyway.

Derek greeted her at the door. He was dressed in a dove-grey suit with white buckskin shoes, a lavender shirt and black knitted tie. He took her into the massive stone room with the windows that came almost down to the level of the water in the mill pond. The day was warm and the windows were open and there was the constant sound of rushing water from the mill-race.

He gave her a dry Martini, so cold it made her teeth ache, and she looked around. The room was sparsely furnished. Along one wall was a refectory table of black oak, on which were several silver dishes, surrounded by half a dozen chairs with leather seats, and a settle. On one wall hung a great shield emblazoned with a design of lilies and leopards and on the wall facing, a battle-axe and a club-headed mace. She had the impression of having wandered on to the movie set of *Hamlet*.

They stood at the open windows while he talked about what he was trying to do with the house, then, after their second Martini, he lifted the lids on the silver dishes and they had a lunch of terrine with black truffles, cold veal and ratatouille, with a Pyrenean cheese and muscat grapes to end. He opened a bottle of Meursault, sniffed it, tasted it, rolled it on his tongue. She was reminded of Georges. It was a meal that suited both the day and the place.

He ate and smoked, sometimes at the same time. He was good-looking in a dark, arrogant way, she thought, and wondered how much of that arrogance had come from being a film star's child.

She asked him about his early childhood in Hollywood. 'I read in one of the newspaper stories that you had grown up on the back lot of Universal.'

'My friends were the children of other actors. We used to play there after the day's shooting had ended.'

'What sort of games?'

'Oh, make-believe. If they had been shooting a western it was easy to believe one was in the Old West. The buildings were there, the street, the hitching-rails. I mean it wasn't running round a suburban garden pointing your finger and going bang-bang! We didn't have to pretend. We had realistic copies of guns which we borrowed from props, and real period clothing. Everything was as real as it could be.'

'And knights?'

'What about them?'

'Did you play at being knights in armour?'

'We may have. I don't remember.'

'But you believed what you were doing, it wasn't really make-believe?'

'We believed. Don't all children?'

'I think most know that they're only pretending.'

'That's no fun.'

When she asked him about the night of the tragedy he moved restlessly from one chair to another and finally stood near the windows, one foot on the sill, looking down at the water a few inches below.

'Tell me,' he said, cutting across her questions, 'why are you doing this?'

'What?'

'This article.'

'Because I was asked to, it's what I do in life. I write for magazines and newspapers.'

'But what interest is there in Great Britain? I mean why do they want to read about an incident in south-western France?'

'Fifteen dead. Half a village wiped out. It's hardly an incident.'

'In August we have more than that killed every day on the roads.'

'Yes, I know, but this is different. I mean, there are personalities involved. Neville for instance. Mr van der Meulen. The villagers. Everyone seems to have suffered some kind of trauma.'

'Don't you think you might be making matters worse? I mean, increasing the trauma. How do you think they will feel seeing your pictures and story now, just when they are getting over the event?'

'I'm sure they're stronger than that. Anyway, they're not likely to see my article. But, look, I don't want to get into an argument with you about the rights or wrongs of journalism. I've been commissioned to do a story and I'm going to do one with or without your help – though, of course, I'd much rather have your help.'

'Tell me what you wish to know,' he said, turning to her so that the light flashed on the dark glasses hiding his eyes.

'Well, tell me about you and Neville, for instance.'

'What about us?'

Inwardly she sighed, this was going to be sticky.

'You've known him a long time?'

'More than ten years. But didn't you ask Mary or Georges about this?'

'They said you had been close. All three of you. And that you had played games about being knights in armour. That you'd pretended to be part of the Age of Chivalry.'

'Go on.'

'I wondered why. I mean what appealed to you about knighthood? Why not cops and robbers, cowboys and Indians? The games you were playing in California?'

'Where do you think those originated? Who do you think kept the peace when peace was necessary, fought the wars when war was necessary? The crusading cop is in a direct line – the very word "crusading" is clear, is it not? And the gunfighter? No more than a knight without armour, holding a modern weapon. Even the "free companies" of knights had their counterparts among the raiders after the American Civil War. Nothing has changed, Miss Bridgman, except there are no longer enough people with a true vision of society.'

He spoke with a force and passion that caused her to frown in puzzlement. 'Did Neville take it as seriously?'

'Both Neville and Pierre.'

'But don't you think that conditions have changed somewhat since the Middle Ages?'

'Famine, disease, and religious superstition were the hallmarks of medieval life: look around you.'

She hastily changed tack. 'What about the night of the tragedy? Mrs Corton said you had been at a disco in Sarlat. You don't look the disco type to me and I wondered—'

'It's all in the papers. Everything about that night.'

'Yes, of course. But I was wondering if there was—'
'*Every*thing.'

She asked several more questions but it was apparent that Derek was not in the mood to answer. Some minutes later she left.

13

'I'm sorry if I'm intruding,' Alex said to van der Meulen as he wheeled a barrow-load of stones down to the river, 'but you're the only person here who was in one of the houses. The only eye-witness.'

He emptied the barrow with a splash and turned back up the slope of rubble. The stones were becoming too big to lift now and he had to break them up with a three-pound hammer and a chisel.

She followed him to the pile and he began to attack one of the pieces of limestone that had smashed down on his house and gone through the roof like a howitzer shell.

She could not speak against the noise and stood waiting for him to finish. It was brutal, she knew, but she had steeled herself. This was the side of journalism she hated, the intrusion into grief, into private feelings. But there was no other way. Thomas van der Meulen had seen everything that night. He was the only observer she had, all the others were dead, everyone else had come just after the catastrophe. Except Neville.

So far van der Meulen had not replied to her questions about that night, treating her as though she wasn't there. Now she asked the question that others had speculated on. 'Mr van der Meulen, what if you find nothing at all under there?'

He stopped, put down the stone he was loading into the barrow and raised his eyes to stare at her. She suddenly realised it was like looking into an empty space. Behind the eyes was nothing. Then slowly he seemed to gather himself.

'But I must,' he said. 'I must speak to her. I must explain. I must ask forgiveness.'

Again Alex followed him down to the water's edge. The stones, just beneath the surface, were forming a kind of groin and the current was sweeping around it, already beginning to change the shape of the bank and creating a small backwater.

'Forgiveness for what?'

He ignored her and wheeled the barrow away from the river.

'Explain what, Mr van der Meulen?'

Suddenly he put the barrow down. 'You have not the right to speak to me; to ask me questions.'

'Of course I have the right. You may not like it, but I have the right.'

She heard footsteps behind her and turned to see Derek Blackwood. He was standing a few paces away, listening. Van der Meulen said, 'You must not ask me more. If you want informations, speak to Georges Corton.'

'All right, I will.'

She turned away and Derek said, 'Good morning, Miss Bridgman.'

He was dressed in his white suit with the panama hat. He looked, she thought, like a Hollywood Frenchman in an old movie.

'Problems?' he said, as they moved out of the way of van der Meulen's barrow.

She shrugged. 'Not really.' She was feeling raw from the interview and did not want to talk to Derek just then.

She turned away and walked down to the river's edge but Derek came with her.

'How is Neville?' he said.

She felt suddenly angry at what was clearly hypocrisy, but kept herself in check. 'About the same.'

'Don't you think it is strange that the only two people who know exactly what happened that night are—?' he put one finger to his temple and twisted it back and forth.

'How do you know Neville's state of mind?'

'How do I – Well, it's apparent, isn't it?' He smiled in a patronising way.

'Apparent to whom?'

'To—'

'Not to you! Or your friend!'

'Miss Bridgman, I'm not sure I understand what—'

'I think it's unforgivable. I mean, they even asked me to go in and talk to Neville in case it might stimulate some sort of reaction. I was glad to do it. But you're his friend and you can't be bothered. As they say, with friends like you who needs enemies.'

She walked swiftly away, leaving Derek where he was, a frown creasing his forehead.

Foto Fournier in Sarlat was near the war memorial. It was a small shop filled with camera equipment. The dark-rooms were at the back.

A middle-aged woman in a white coat was behind the counter. Alex handed her the receipt for the rolls of film she had brought in, collected the envelopes, and took them to the bar near the cathedral where she could look at the transparencies against the bright sky.

She couldn't make out the first few at all. She could see foliage and sky but that was about all. Then, when she looked more closely, she saw in each picture one or more birds. She did not know much about birds but could recognise a heron wading in shallow water in one transparency and several ducks on a pond, or it may have been a little bay on a river. Another showed a duck with a flotilla of ducklings streaming out behind it.

These were certainly not hers. She scratched about in her handbag and found a photographic receipt. It was in her name. She realised what had happened. She had handed in the receipt she had found in Petit Louis' torch by mistake and now had his bird pictures, which Max had told her about.

She finished her coffee and went back to the shop. She explained to the woman what seemed to have gone wrong. Madame Fournier looked in several drawers, then she excused herself, went through a door that led to the rear of the building and Alex heard her shouting, 'Jean-Claude!'

There was a low rumble of a man's voice, then she returned looking agitated and said, 'My husband will attend to you in a minute.'

Monsieur Fournier was a thin man, almost bald, with angry flashing eyes. 'How can I help you?' he said, in the way the French had, Alex thought, of being so icily polite as to be insulting.

She explained again. Before she had finished he nodded his head angrily. 'Yes. Yes. I remember. The gentleman said some of the pictures were not processed well. He said he had used a laboratory in Périgueux but would use us in future if our work merited it.'

He went to another drawer and pulled out an envelope. 'This was his third roll. The one I was supposed to "improve". It was impossible. You have the other two. Come, I will show you.'

There was a viewer screen to the left of the counter. He took several of the transparencies from the envelope, clipped them on to the screen and switched on the light. 'Please look. Here. Do you see? It is so black.'

All of them had massive black patches in the foreground, outlined by a thin jagged tangerine line. She had seen photographs of an eclipse of the sun which looked similar.

'I mean if you take an image against a strong light what can you expect but a black silhouette? I am not God. I cannot change things to get more detail. That is what he wanted me to do. Bring up details of the silhouette. I tell you that the silhouette is burnt on to the emulsion.'

Angrily he gathered up the transparencies and pushed them into the envelope and returned to the back of the counter.

Alex said, 'You said this was the third roll, but I only have one. The one with the bird pictures on it.'

'He took one with him,' Madame Fournier said. 'I remember now.'

'So that is that,' her husband said. He nodded to Alex and went back to his work. Madame Fournier watched him go, half in apprehension, half in relief.

Alex paid her for her own pictures and Madame Fournier said, 'And these? Who will pay for these?'

A look of fiscal apprehension passed over her face. It was an expression Alex had seen on the faces of many shopkeepers in many countries at the thought of a financial loss.

Alex paid and took the envelope to the car and looked at the transparencies again. Monsieur Fournier was right. There was nothing he could have done about the black images in the foreground. In some they looked like ink smudges, in others she thought she could make out human shapes. Heads. Some angular projections that might have been arms.

Towards the end of the series she came to one which seemed to be the figure of a man standing in front of a bush, a small branch broke the outline of his profile.

She drove back to Carriac, parked in the little car park and went for a drink at the hotel. Dr Max was in his khaki dust-coat, investigating the base of the cliff. Van der Meulen was loading his barrow with stones. She did not want to speak to either of them just then.

It was a brilliantly sunny day, with heat radiating from the stone of the terrace, and she sat under a Noilly Prat sun umbrella and drank an Ancre Pils.

It was the kind of day she should be with David. They should be having a beer together, then a long and sensual lunch, something cold, like lobster, with a bottle of Pouilly-Fumé in an ice bucket and wild strawberries with kirsch to follow. Then they would go up to their bedroom, close the shutters and, in the warm half-light, make love until they were exhausted.

She could almost pretend that such a scene was possible. That everything was normal. Almost. Except for the rubble and the demolished houses and the fact that of the two figures she could see, one was looking for the carcase of an ancient rhinoceros and the other for the bones of his wife.

14

The afternoon turned hot. It was the kind of heat that Alex remembered from her childhood. She worked at her notes for a while and then changed into a swimsuit and walked down to the little *plage* which lay about two hundred metres downstream of the Corton house.

The *plage* was no more than a long pebbly bank which would have been flooded when the river was in spate. Now there was a small kiosk on it selling ice creams, fizzy drinks, sandwiches, merguez sausages and crêpes; and renting umbrellas, back-rests and straw mats.

Normally, at this time of year, the beach would have been well patronised. But the rockfall had caused a blight and there were barely half a dozen groups sunning themselves.

As a child she had always been made to wear yellow plastic sandals by her mother, who feared broken glass. Now she would not have been caught dead in them and hobbled over the stones trying to find a patch of sand to lie on.

She sunbathed for nearly an hour and all that time she managed to keep her thoughts at bay, consciously trying to relax. Instead of thinking of what she might be uncovering in Carriac, she remembered instead the last time she and David had been alone together.

He was a marvellous lover, she thought. He suited

her. The chemistry was right. He had only to caress her and she was instantly aroused. It was something she had known about him instinctively, even before they went to bed together.

On that very first day, walking round Hyde Park, full of grilled lamb and Château Musar, she knew that if he had wanted to take her to a hotel she would have gone right then. But she was glad he hadn't, pleased he had taken her to his home instead.

They had, in fact, taken some weeks to consummate their affair, not through any foot-dragging on either part but because of circumstances.

When he left her at her flat that first night he had kissed her lightly on the forehead and said, 'See you tomorrow.'

But she had not seen him the following day, for his secretary had phoned saying he had had to fly suddenly to Australia where their subsidiary company was facing a financial crisis.

He had been away for ten days. He had phoned her from Sydney, apologising and telling her when he would be back and making another date.

This time it was she who had had to write him a note saying she would be in Scotland for a week on a story. She had phoned him from Inverness.

'If I was superstitious I'd say that the omens were against us,' he had said.

'Are you?'

'Absolutely not.'

'That's good. Nor am I. I'll be back on Friday. Let me make you dinner.' There had been a fractional pause. 'I'm a good cook,' she had said defensively. Now, of course, she realised he had been thinking of Simon.

'Terrific. I'll supply the wine.'

She had got back too late to prepare a complicated meal so she had dashed out to the Finchley Road and come back with frozen *moules* and a couple of steaks. She'd made a green salad, bathed and changed – and then the phone had rung. Simon was sick, some kind of gastric bug.

She had stood for a few moments looking at the candles and the festive table, the tray of drinks. She thought of the mussels and the steaks in the fridge. She wasn't hungry. Instead she poured herself a mammoth gin and tonic, took a large swallow and said, 'What about a lovely evening with the telly, dear?'

At nine-thirty, just when she was considering the proposition of pouring a third gin, the phone rang. It was David. 'Simon's much better and he's asleep. Sally says she can sit. Is ten o'clock too late to eat?'

'Let's try it.'

They ate the mussels and the steaks and drank a bottle of Australian shiraz. He told her about his trip and she told him about Scotland and when they had finished their coffee he said, 'I think I'm in love with you. If being unable to get you out of my mind even on the other side of the world is anything to go by then I'm pretty sure. But I have to warn you, I'm a sexual maniac.'

She had stood up and he had risen with her and put his arms around her. 'Just so long as you confine your ravings to me,' she had said.

Now, lying near the big green river, she felt restless at the memory. Why couldn't things have gone on like that? Why were there always other people to take into account?

She swam in water that smelled slightly of earth and was towelling herself when a voice said, 'Bonjour, Alex. You swim like a champion.' It was Max Wellmann and he was holding out a bottle of Orangina. 'Join me?' She took it gratefully.

He brought with him a different set of stimuli. David vanished and was replaced by the burnt house, the rockfall, the bodies.

'How are you getting on?' he said.

'The more questions I ask, the more there are.'

'What do you need to know?'

'Everything. I feel as though I'm sitting in a car on a wet day with the windows misted up. I can't see clearly the objects I know are there.'

'Go on. I'll try.'

'Well, Petit Louis. I've seen his house. And I know who he was, but that's about all. I don't have any flesh for his bones.'

'Ah, Petit Louis.'

'He's one of the most important characters in the story, don't you think?'

Max was wearing a floppy white sun-hat, white shorts above thick knotted legs and a dark blue sports shirt. The hat shaded his pock-marked face and he looked away from her to the turbid green water.

After a moment's silence he said, 'I suppose you get a Petit Louis in many of these village communities. A person who doesn't fit in. I told you that physically he was very strong but he was misshapen and country people are . . . I was going to say superstitious but uneasy might be a better word.'

'You make them sound medieval. Carriac's a sophisticated place.'

'Only in the last thirty or forty years. Only since outsiders began to come. Before that this whole area, like the Massif Central and the Languedoc, retained a kind of remoteness. Go into Haute Provence sometime, or the Massif des Maures, and you'll see what I mean.

'On the surface Petit Louis was someone from the village just like anyone else. But below the surface there were the old superstitions. I've seen people cross themselves when he came into a shop.'

'Did you know him well?'

'No one knew him well. I was in Buenos Aires when he was a child, so I only got to know him when he was in his teens.'

She looked surprised. 'I thought he would have been much older than that.'

'He was only a few years older than Neville. In fact, when they were children he used to play with them.'

'You surprise me again.'

'The boys grew up together. All of them. Pierre, Derek and Neville – and Louis. That cottage you saw was the family home. Louis' father disappeared years ago. No one knows why, it may have been because his son was deformed. He didn't leave a note. He was last seen on the road to Bordeaux and has never been heard of since.

'His mother, Jeanette Seurel, cleaned and ironed to make ends meet. When Louis was a little boy she had to take him with her. She cleaned for Mary Corton and for the Chervases and for a few families in the village. Petit Louis would play with the children of the families while his mother did the work.'

'He played with Neville?'

'And the other two.'

'The knights-in-armour games?'

'Those too. Mary told me how those developed. When we played cowboys and Indians in the old days we always used to look for someone to tie up, someone to be the Indian.'

'Let me guess. Wasn't it usually someone's sister?'

'I'm afraid it was. Someone weaker than we were.

This is what happened in their games. They'd let Petit Louis play because they needed a bad knight, a black knight, the knight who did not uphold the laws of chivalry, someone whom they could destroy.

'They would hold "tournaments" and each in turn would fight Petit Louis. He must have been eleven or twelve when I first came here. His mother used to clean for me, too. One day she asked me to have a look at him. I found extensive bruising on his chest where he had been struck by their wooden lances.'

'How long did this go on?'

'Several years.'

'Why did he put up with it, he didn't have to play with them?'

'These were children of the wealthy. He was the son of the poorest in the village. Can you imagine what it did for him; the food he ate, the luxury that rubbed off on him, the presents he received from parents who were worried about how he was being treated by their children? It wasn't easy to give it up.

'But then, as is the way of these associations, the boys grew up, went to boarding school, saw Petit Louis a few times when they came back, but the "friendship" did not survive.'

'My God, boys can be horrible!'

'Not all boys. Derek was the problem. It was Derek who made him into the enemy, the infidel. And when he wasn't the enemy he was a kind of servant, fetching and carrying. Derek doesn't seem aware of the changes that have taken place in the world.'

'Perhaps he doesn't *want* to be aware of them.'

It was night and the candles were lit. The air was heavy with the smell of incense and marijuana. Derek and Pierre sat at either end of the refectory table in the mill-house. They'd eaten a meal of wild duck and rice and the debris still littered the table. With that they had drunk three bottles of Mercurey and were now drinking Armagnac.

'I can't see it,' Pierre was saying.

'Why not? All that "nobility" shit? You're not a little boy any more and Georges isn't the king. You remember how he was *always* the king . . . and the kissing of his hands . . . and the swearing of fealty . . . ? Well, not now.'

'But you can't be certain. You don't know for sure.'

'Jesus, even you should be able to work it out. I tell you the journalist was angry. She thinks we're bastards because we haven't been to see him. Now who would have told her that? Not Neville. So it's his mother or Georges. So who's kept us away from him?'

'Georges.'

'Right.'

'But why? He couldn't know what happened.'

Derek fitted a cigarette into his holder. The room was hot even though the windows were open. Pierre's shirt was unbuttoned. Derek was dressed in a long black and white caftan.

'Not unless Neville has started to talk.'

Pierre said, 'Even if he was okay he wouldn't talk. It's just as bad for him.'

'Neville blabbed about everything. You know that.'

He gave them each another Armagnac then rose and walked over to the window. He placed an oil lamp on the sill and looked down into the clear water. Two trout came lazily up to the light and he dropped in pieces of meat. The fish went for them hungrily.

'One day they will turn cannibal and begin to eat each other,' Derek said.

'What are we going to do?'

'We're going to watch him and we're going to ask him why.'
'Maybe he wants money. They say his wife's got it all.'
'Georges hasn't got a sou. She gives him everything. He spends it on whores in Paris. Neville told me.'
'Not only whores. I heard my mother telling my father. She said he would try it with anyone.'
'You wonder how a worm like Georges knows so much about chivalry.'
'And yet we believed him. We idolised him.'
'Of course we did. But only when we were small. Anyway, it doesn't matter how you learn these things, provided they're true. I mean the fact that Georges talks about nobility doesn't make it ridiculous. It just makes him ridiculous.'
'And then?'
'Then what?'
'Say he's figured it out?'
'Then we deal with him. I don't pay blackmailers.'
Pierre looked uncomfortable.
'What's the matter? Don't you have the stomach?'
'It's like a chain reaction. Something happens which causes something else to happen and so on. When does it *stop*?'
'When I say it stops.'

15

'I'm supposed to talk to you, Neville, in the hope that I can jog your memory and that that in turn will start you talking,' Alex said. 'But I've begun to wonder if just talking about this and that is enough. Something stronger, maybe.'

They were in Neville's room and she had decided to take a tougher line as an experiment. The morning sun was striking the house and already the day was hot. The electronic screen lay still and blank on his knees. Sire Geoffroy de Charny, Sire Baudouin d'Annequin and the Count of Dammartin were lost in a mindless limbo.

'I once did a story about psychiatric shocks. You know, the ones they give people with manic depression. ECT it's called.'

She watched his face. He sat in the deep shade of the shutters and she could not see his eyes. Music throbbed on the CD and she turned it down.

'Electro-convulsive therapy. You must have heard of it. People were worried about it for a long time, Neville, because it seemed to twist your body into knots and produce terrific pain. But it doesn't any more because they give you an anaesthetic first.

'Well, when I was doing research for that story I found out that long, long ago, nearly two thousand years ago, doctors were giving patients shocks by making them touch those fish called electric rays. And even in the seventeenth century they were blindfolding people and pouring ice-cold water over them.

'That's why I'm going to talk about Petit Louis. His name's my electric shock. It was so brave of you to try and save him. I wonder why you didn't save him long ago.'

The screen jumped into life. Plink... plink... plink...

'That's okay, Neville, you play the game if it comforts you. What was I... oh, yes... I was wondering whether you'd ever tried to help Petit Louis when he was a child. He used to play those knightly games with you and Derek and Pierre, didn't he? Cowboys and Indians in armour. And wasn't he the one you tied up or the one you bruised or terrified in one way or another? Didn't you bully him and make his life intolerable?'

He was staring down at the game, his fingers hitting the buttons, but he was not concentrating, she could tell that.

'I'm no psychiatrist. I don't really know much about it except what I picked up doing my story and, of course, what one picks up reading and just living. But I'm wondering if there isn't a question of guilt here, Neville.'

She was sitting forward, trying to see his eyes. He swung the chair away as though realising this.

'No, don't.' She gripped the arm, touching his wrist as she did so. He jerked away. 'It's all right,' she said, soothingly. 'I'm not going to hurt you. I just want to see your face. You don't mind, do you? I don't like talking to people's backs.'

But she left the chair where it was and moved her own. She still could not see his eyes.

'You see, Neville, I've been doing some digging and I've found out about Petit Louis and who he was and how he came to be here. And I began to wonder about guilt.

'Just say that someone had been cruel to a boy who was poor and misshapen and then years later had failed to save that boy when he was trapped by a rockfall. It's just possible, isn't it, that the one who had been cruel might have been carrying a load of guilt that was suddenly released? I mean, he'd failed to save him, failed to make up for his earlier cruelty.'

She rose and stood by the window. 'What do you think, Neville? No? Well, it was only a theory.'

She walked slowly round the room picking up things. She picked up his CDs and looked at them. Picked up a car magazine, flipped through the pages. He moved the chair so that he could watch her.

'Is this the famous cupboard?'

She was standing in front of a closed wall-cupboard about six feet high and three feet wide.

'Your mother told me about this cupboard.'

Neville moved the chair forward.

'This is where you keep your secret things, isn't it? The ones for your eyes only? I'd like to see them, Neville.'

Slowly the chair came nearer.

'I'll just . . . '

She caught one of the cupboard handles and began to push it down.

She saw how he tensed himself in the chair, pushing up on the arm rests. God, she thought, he's going to jump at me!

He opened his mouth. She waited. He drew breath into his lungs.

There was a knock at the door and Mary Corton entered. 'How're you getting on?' she said. Neville sank back into his chair, turned and faced the windows. Alex gave a slight shrug and Mary nodded understandingly. 'What about some coffee?' she said.

'Bonjour, Thomas,' Georges Corton said. 'Hard at it?'

The Dutchman ignored him. He broke up a piece of limestone and placed the bits in his barrow. Most of the cliff rock had been removed now and he was starting on the weathered grey stone of his house. Pieces of timber stuck out like broken bones.

Georges looked over his shoulder but the only people in sight were outside the *boulangerie* about a hundred metres away. They were deep in their own conversation.

'I've told you before, Thomas. It's important. Very important for you. Don't you understand? Especially as you're a fellow Mason. I don't want you to get into trouble.'

Van der Meulen pushed the barrow past him and emptied it into the river.

'Listen, I know the journalist was talking to you. I saw her. What did she want? Did you show her anything? Have you found anything?'

Van der Meulen trundled the barrow up the slope with Georges at his side.

'I've told you, Thomas, not once but a dozen times – you find anything you show me! Understand?'

Van der Meulen looked at him, seemed about to say something and then closed his mouth.

'Thomas,' Georges said softly. 'Here you're among friends. We understand your problems. But to other people you may seem . . . a little deranged. And you know what they do with mad people? They lock them up, Thomas, and throw away the key.'

Van der Meulen put down his barrow and stared at Georges.

'It's true, Thomas. And you wouldn't like that. Especially if I told them what you did to Marie.' Georges left him there and went to the Mercedes parked under the plane-trees. He drove to the Harris house, opened the gates and parked the car out of sight of the road. He looked about him carefully. Everything was still. Nothing moved. The only sound was the far-off thrum of a motorbike engine. He took the path through the bamboo to Petit Louis' cottage.

He had been before and had searched it thoroughly but now, as he slipped the padlock on the door and pushed it open, he could see that others had been after him. They had also searched thoroughly, brutally might be the word. Georges had replaced everything the way it was. But whoever had come after him had not cared about such niceties. Coir from the mattress littered the bedroom floor. Papers, magazines, pots and pans, were strewn everywhere, drawers had been pulled open, their contents spilled.

He stood in the deep and gloomy silence of the room and looked about. What would be the point of searching this rubbish? Whoever it was would have found it by now, that's if it was here, and if whoever it was knew what he or she was looking for.

What he wanted to know was: WHY?

Alex and Mary had finished their coffee and were in the tower room. They had discussed again the circumstances surrounding the tragic night, then Alex said, 'I don't think I'm making any headway with Neville.'

'It's been good of you to try.'

'I'm surprised that Derek and Pierre haven't come to see him. They're the obvious ones.'

Mary shook her head angrily. 'Georges has asked them several times. I would have gone to them myself except that we've had our problems and they've always adored Georges. It's cruel. But then Derek always has been odd.'

Alex waited for her to continue and when she did not she prompted her by describing her lunch with Derek.

'What did you think of his house?'

'It's going to be very atmospheric when it's finished.'

'Was he wearing his caftan?'

'No.'

'He's taken to wearing one at home. He says it's how the Crusaders dressed after they'd lived for some years in the Holy Land. Gone native, we'd call it today.'

'I suppose we all have our fantasies.'

'His whole life has been built on fantasy. First his mother's and then his.'

Mary gave them each more coffee. 'Do you know anything about his mother?' she asked.

'Just that she was an actress. Several marriages.'

'I did some research on her once. I thought I'd use her in a novel, but she was too real for my kind of fiction. She was a working-class girl from Lyons with big boobs, a small waist and long sexy legs. First she was a photographer's model, then a pin-up, and then she was, quote, discovered, and acted in half a dozen soft porn movies before taking the trail to Hollywood.'

'I seem to have heard this one before,' Alex said.

'A dozen times. But that doesn't make it any less real. Contracts had been waved in front of her and promises made, but once she got out there it was difficult to find work. She started sleeping with anyone who could pay the bills. Then she married a TV producer and started getting small parts in day-time soaps. He was Derek's father. That didn't last long. The point is all of his friends were Hollywood kids, most of them rich, most of them spoiled.'

Alex remembered her conversation with Max but decided not to mention it.

'I suppose that's where he learned to fantasise,' Alex said.

'It's not difficult to understand if your parents are in the business. You play where they work. Apparently he loved guns, used to borrow them from props. Anyway, they must have gone to his head because he shot one of his mother's lovers. He may well have thought that the gun was a "prop" gun – the sort he played with. But it was real enough. She kept it in her bedside cabinet.'

Alex itched for paper and pencil but knew if she took down anything she might break the flow.

Mary was staring into space over the top of her coffee cup. She went on, 'Apparently he heard his mother and her lover having a fight in the lounge, so he went upstairs and got the gun and shot the man.

'He was a small-time actor, ten or twelve years younger than Julia Berri and supposed to be an unsavoury character with a history of violence towards women. So when Derek's lawyer made out a case that Derek was only defending his mother it never even went to trial.

'It was the sort of publicity that Julia needed, not in the States, but over here. It made her. She came back to France and made a dozen or more movies here and in Italy, then married an industrialist. They died when his plane crashed on the way to the Le Mans Twenty-Four Hour Race a few years ago.

'That left Derek with enough money never to have to worry. Which is a pity. I believe people should work. Don't you?'

Alex thought of Georges and Neville and Pierre and even Max Wellmann and then said, 'Oh yes. Yes, I do.'

That evening Alex changed her formula. Instead of dining in the village she drove along the river to La Roque-Gageac and ate on the outside terrace of the Gardette. The weather was hot and close and she could see lightning flashing above the River Lot forty miles to the south.

She was the only person dining alone. At first she wanted to hurry and get the meal over with but then she became irritated with herself. She was often away on stories by herself, she often dined alone, this was no different – except that she should have been in Brittany, dining with David.

She forced herself to take her time and after she had finished stood for half an hour watching a game of boules under floodlights. It was nearly eleven o'clock by the time she was driving back along the river. She entered Carriac on the opposite side to the Cortons' house. The single track road through the village was closed for the night and in the dark she could not see the small lane around the back of the village that Georges Corton had shown her, so she parked under the plane-trees in the little public car park.

She sat in the car for a few minutes gathering her courage. She had to walk through the empty village as she had done the night before. But nothing had happened to her then and, she told herself, nothing would happen to her now. In any case *there was no other way.*

She locked the car, took off her shoes because her feet had swollen in the heat, and began to walk along the *quai*.

As she approached the area of the rockfall she saw

a light near the base of the cliff where the fracture had occurred. The light swung backwards and forwards, then side to side, its beam playing on the rubble. It picked out van der Meulen's wheelbarrow, then part of a wall.

She stopped. Someone was clearly looking for something, but since the villagers were often on the piles of rubble, turning over stones, hunting for personal belongings, she did not think it strange.

She was about to go forward when she realised that something ahead, only a matter of a dozen or so metres, had moved. She stood quite still on her bare feet and stared into the darkness.

Pieces of ruined buildings were faintly silhouetted against the street lights at the far end of the village, but they were angular and jagged, this shape was rounded. It moved again and she realised it was a man with his back to her.

Above him the light, like a firefly, jumped from one place to the next and Alex realised that the man was watching the person at the base of the cliff.

Who will watch the watchers?

The light began to descend the sloping pile of rubble. She sensed that the man in front of her would move back. Before he could do so she ran swiftly along the road on silent feet and did not stop until she reached the driveway of the Cortons' house.

In the village the light bobbed over the rubble and the watcher watched. As the light came closer the watcher said, 'Bon soir, Georges.'

'My God! Who's that? Pierre? God, you gave me a fright! What the hell are you doing here?'

'Looking for you. And I may ask the same.'

'I was talking to Thomas earlier. Or trying to. And I

lost a cufflink. One of my gold ones. At least I think I lost it here.'

Georges was a large man but Pierre made him look small.

'What do you want, anyway?' Georges said.

'Derek would like to see you.'

'I'll go round tomorrow.'

'No, now.'

'Don't be silly. I'm not going down that lane at this time. It's all mud.'

'He said I should tell you he has a bottle of Montrachet '71. Two bottles in fact.'

'What! Good heavens, I haven't seen one for years.'

'He found them at Grenuier's in Brive.'

'What did he pay?'

'Don't ask. He said to tell you he put them on ice forty-five minutes ago. Will you come?'

'Of course. Even if I have to crawl down the lane on my hands and knees.'

16

Alex found sleep difficult. She switched off the light, then switched it back on again after half an hour's tossing and turning. She did some work. She yawned. She put out the light. But in the darkness sleep fled and she lay wide awake, her mind flicking from one thought to the next.

Who had been watching the man on the rubble? And what had he been looking for?

The shape of her article began to form in her head. Robin Akers had asked her for a piece reporting how a community was coping with the aftermath of disaster. But this was different. It was like a kind of amoebic growth. Each time you thought you were holding the main story in your head a piece separated and began growing and producing a new crop of questions. She had many more questions now than she had answers.

Still uneasy, she remembered the torch. She had bought batteries in Sarlat but when she tried to fit them they were fractionally too big and would not go in. She needed to go to the bank the following day and she would take the torch in then and get the right ones.

Finally she slept.

Along the passage from her the movie on TV came to an end. Neville switched down the sound as the ads came on and switched up the volume on the CD player, then he wheeled his chair to the window and stared out into the velvety dark.

He didn't hear the music just as he hadn't taken in much of the movie. His mind was still churning with the thoughts of the last session he had had with the journalist.

She had touched on things that only a few people knew. His mother. His step-father. They wouldn't have told her. Who then?

Swear.

He could hear Derek's voice as clear as a bell over the years. They would have been ten or eleven then, Petit Louis a couple of years older. But he never *seemed* older. If anything he seemed younger.

They had gone up into the hills, just the four of them: Derek, Petit Louis, Pierre and himself. They had a house up there, not a real house, but a kind of cave, a jumble of rocks that formed the walls of a room. Pierre had found it one day when he was shooting pigeons.

They had cut reeds and made a roof and often went up there on days when the heat was excessive near the river. There was a flat rock against one wall. They pretended it was a throne. Of course Derek had sat there most of the time.

He would be Sire de Charny and they would offer fealty to him, kneeling before him and placing their hands between his and repeating the phrase, 'Sire, I become thy man.'

Neville had always wondered – had indeed checked with Georges – about the Count of Dammartin having to swear loyalty and Georges had said he would not have done so, would never even have been asked, but Neville had not the nerve to refuse Derek. Nor had Pierre.

But Petit Louis had. He had never questioned anything before, had been only too glad to play whatever rôle Derek assigned him. But then Derek had sat on the 'throne' one day and shown them a small piece of wood and had said it was a splinter of the True Cross and that they must now swear upon this holy relic.

It was an ordinary piece of wood, the kind of splinter that might have come from a builder's plank. Neville had no objection, nor Pierre. They had both taken the splinter in their hands and sworn.

But Petit Louis had said no. It was well known in the village that his mother was devout. He did not believe they should play games like that. It was bad luck.

Swear.

But he had remained obdurate.

That was when Derek had called him an infidel.

It was only a step to the next stage. Petit Louis wasn't sure what they were doing, for Derek had whispered his instructions to the other two, so that when they came for Petit Louis and tied his hands behind his back he was frightened and had protested that he had to go home.

But Derek had tied him to a young tree and piled faggots – he had said this was the correct word – around the base of the tree and had set them alight.

The grass beneath the wood was very dry. It had gone up suddenly, with a whoosh, and by the time they had kicked the burning faggots away and managed to get Petit Louis untied, his trousers had caught alight and the skin on his legs had blistered badly.

There had been hell to pay. Money had changed hands, apologies were made, hospital bills paid, punishments meted out.

It was the last time Petit Louis had played with them.

But the point was that everything had been hushed up. Louis' mother, Madame Seurel, knew of course, and so did the other parents, but no one else.

So if Neville's own mother and step-father had not told the English journalist – and why should they? – then it had to be Derek or Pierre. And Pierre wouldn't. Neville was sure of that. So it had to be Derek.

But why?

He flicked on the electronic game. Plink-plonk... plink-plonk...

He thought and thought but he could not come to any conclusion. And then he remembered what she had said about guilt. Was it true? Could it be true? Is that why he was where he was and like he was?

Guilt?

The following morning was hot by eight o'clock and Alex decided to get Sarlat over with early, come back, work, then swim.

She returned to the shop in the long main street where she had bought the batteries and told the young man that she much regretted it but she had bought the wrong ones. Did he remember her? Could she change them?

Every so often Alex was made aware that she was an attractive woman and not part of an aggressive unisex population where all were equal under God.

The man, about her own age, took on the rôle of the gallant Frenchman dealing with a beautiful damsel in distress. He even – and this surprised her – spoke English.

'I remember you well,' he said, sounding like Maurice Chevalier.

'I tried to put them in but... perhaps I was too

clumsy.' She adapted to the rôle model he offered.
'May I?' He took the torch from her and unscrewed the base. He pressed a battery into the tube. It stuck. He frowned.
'But they are the correct ones,' he said. 'One moment.' He unscrewed the lamp holder and the reflector and held the tube up to the light. 'Yes. I see. It seems there is a blockage.' He inserted a pair of long white fingers and gently pulled out what looked like a piece of plastic. Then another, and another. Until there were five or six photographic transparencies lying on his counter.

With a long finger he scraped out the small pieces of glue which had been holding them there, slipped the batteries into the torch, screwed in the reflector, bulb holder and the base and switched on. The light was brilliant.

She thanked him and left the shop. She turned into a side street and held the transparencies up to the sky. They were like the others, but closer, clearer. The tangerine line flickered and flared, and there was something else she could not make out.

She hurried to the photographic shop. Madame Fournier eyed her with a look that said, 'You have come to make trouble.' But when Alex asked if she could see the transparencies on the viewing machine the woman waved at it with relief and said, 'Certainly. You know how to switch it on?'

Alex placed the six transparencies on the machine and switched on the light behind them.

'Madame, do you have a magnifying glass?'
'Of course.'

She held the glass to her eye and examined each one in turn. When she had finished she was shaking.

125

She bought the magnifying glass, put the transparencies in the side pocket of her handbag and stumbled out into the street. Her car was parked some distance down the road and the interior was boiling. She sat in it for some minutes with the windows open, unaware of the perspiration forming on her forehead, then she took out the transparencies and looked at them once again, holding them against the front windscreen and moving the glass very slowly over each picture.

Thomas van der Meulen was late getting to his work. He saw a counsellor twice a week at the apartment he was staying at in Souillac. Several of the survivors were still seeing counsellors, especially those who had lost loved ones.

The counsellor, who came from Périgueux, was a man some ten years younger than Thomas and after all these weeks had made little in-road into the post-shock trauma which the middle-aged Dutchman was suffering. Time, the counsellors said to each other at their weekly meetings, time was eventually on their side.

So it was a little past ten o'clock on this boiling morning when Thomas began to pile his bits of cliff and bits of house into the wheelbarrow and trundle it down to the river.

The bank, where he tipped, was in deep shade at this time of the morning and so at first he did not see the body. The rush and splash of the stones created wavelets and the wavelets caused the body to move up and down in the reeds where it floated face down, arms supported by the water.

At first Thomas thought it was the body of an animal, a calf or a goat that had been washed downstream – which sometimes happened in stormy weather. But there had not been a storm for some time and even in

Thomas' blurred mind the fact began to establish itself that this was a human being and that the human being was dead.

It was like an electric shock. He stopped. The mists cleared for a moment. He knew where he was and what he had to do. He dropped the wheelbarrow and ran along the road to the *gendarme* controlling the single line of traffic.

In a quiet landscape a running figure spells trouble. By the time Thomas had reached the policeman, people at the far end of the village who were coming out of the supermarket had already spotted him.

The policeman said, 'For the hundredth time, Monsieur van der Meulen, there is *no* body under the house. We found your wife. She is buried!'

'No, no, not my wife. A man's body. In the river.'

Thomas ran back along the *quai* followed by the *gendarme*. The shoppers began to hurry in the same direction.

Alex, on her way back from Sarlat, parked her car by the hotel and followed them. Her mind was still churning with what she had seen on the transparencies, and she had only wanted to get to her room, lock the door, and sit down and think. Now she followed the group of women.

The bank was steep. Thomas went down with the *gendarme*. Everyone craned to look. The policeman, standing up to his thighs in the water, caught the body and pulled it from the reeds. He turned it over. There was a gasp from everyone. It was Georges.

Alex felt her stomach twist and turn. 'Oh, no,' she said out loud, but no one seemed to hear her. The faces of the women were horrified but fascinated.

Van der Meulen cut steps in the earth bank with his spade then helped the *gendarme* to lift Georges out of the water and carry him on to the road. His face looked like butcher's meat.

Alex knew she had to get away from the place. She fought her way out of the now growing crowd. She began to feel faint.

'Please let me through!'

She felt hands grip her arms.

She struggled. 'Let me through!'

A voice said, 'It's all right. I've got you.' She felt herself lifted and carried to the shade of the plane-trees.

'You'll feel better in a few moments.'

The voice was familiar. She opened her eyes. It was David.

17

'You sounded so miserable on the phone the other night I couldn't sleep for hours worrying about you,' David said.

'I'm glad it wasn't just the awful weather that made you come south.'

'Of course it wasn't. Simon thought it was a good idea, too.'

They were sitting on the shaded terrace of the Gardette in La Roque-Gageac. David and his son had arrived late the night before and Simon was still asleep.

She stretched out her hand and covered his. 'I'm glad to see you! I don't know what I—' She broke off.

'You've had a hell of a shock. Let me get you another cognac.'

She shook her head. 'I'm not used to drinking cognac in the morning. Anyway, I must be getting back. I can't go on staying at the Cortons' now.'

'I'll book you in here.'

'When I first arrived all these hotels were supposed to be full. That's what I was told, anyway.'

'Well, they've got vacancies now. I'll go and root Simon out.' He half rose.

Suddenly she did not want to go back to Carriac, not yet anyway. Instead she said, 'Could I have a coffee?'

Just being with David seemed to relax her; she was

no longer alone; this was how it should always be, she thought.

'Do you want to talk about it?' he said.

'No. Not now. Not . . . ' And then it all came pouring out in an unstoppable flood. She told him everything that had happened, repeating details she had already described on the phone, bringing everything up to date, to the moment she had seen Georges' body floating in the river.

He listened in silence, his thin face cocked to one side, the smoke from his cigarette curling up past his eyes.

When she finished she found that he was holding her hand and that her nails had dug into his skin. He had endured the pain without moving a muscle.

'Let's see the transparencies,' he said.

She brought them out of her bag and gave them to him with the magnifying glass. He held them up to the blue sky and examined each in turn. 'And you think this is the what's-their-names' house?'

'Harris.'

She took one of the transparencies. The story they told was all plain now, quite unlike the first series she had seen. There the tangerine line had looked more like an eclipse of the sun than a house fire. She could imagine what must have happened. Petit Louis must have seen the glow in the sky from his cottage, picked up his camera and run along the path through the bamboo.

'And then he started taking pictures with a zoom lens. You can see that there are some wide-angle shots and some close-ups. But even with the telephoto he was too far away and I suppose shrubs and trees got in the way. But then he got closer and look!'

'What?'

'Don't you see? Here, take the glass.'

He focused the magnifying glass where her finger was pointing. It was on one of the upstairs windows of the Harris house. The building was ablaze and there were flames in all the rooms.

'What am I supposed to be looking at?' Through the glass he could see what looked like two black sticks in an open V formation. 'The things that look like—?'

'Sticks. Only they're not.'

'What do you think they are?'

'Arms.'

'Arms?' He looked more closely. 'Whose?'

'I think they belong to either Mr or Mrs Harris.'

'Jesus!'

'I think we're seeing someone's cry for help. Look how the arms are spread. It's just what anyone would do if they were trapped in a burning house.'

He stared for a long moment at the transparency, unwilling to believe her.

'But—'

'Look, we know the Harrises died in the house.'

'Upstairs?'

'No idea, but why not? That's where the bedrooms usually are. And if Dr Wellmann is right and someone set fire to the house deliberately—'

'That's only *his* idea.'

'Let me show you something else.' She dug in her bag until she came up with the first envelope of transparencies. 'Look at this.' She was pointing to the rounded silhouettes which almost blocked off the house and fire.

'I don't—'

'That looks like a head, doesn't it? It's the right shape.'

'Except for this black line sticking out the side of it!'

131

'Could be a twig. But doesn't the rest of it look like a head?'

'Okay.'

'Well, then this whole mass of silhouette could be two or more people standing together. Petit Louis must have taken his pictures from behind them, shooting towards the fire.'

'Why would he do that? I mean, if he wanted to photograph the fire and if he was as good as you say he was, he'd have gone to a different position.'

'But what if he wanted to photograph the fire *and* the people?'

'He'd shoot from the front. Let the fire illuminate the faces. That's what I'd do anyway.'

'Not if you didn't want to be seen.'

He paused and then said, 'Wow!'

'Wow is right.'

They stared at each other and Alex felt the prickling of certainty at the base of her neck.

David stared past her and his face broke into a welcoming smile. 'Sleep well?' he said.

Simon joined them. He put out his hand and Alex shook it formally. He stared at her, his eyes going right through her. She had forgotten how steady and penetrating those eyes could be.

'I'm glad you came,' she said. 'The weather's much better down here.'

He did not reply and she wondered just how happy he was at having his holiday plans changed.

And then, as he moved to take a chair, she saw Pierre Chervas sitting on the far side of the terrace. When they had arrived they were the only people there. She wondered how long he had been there. He was drinking coffee and staring at her over the rim of the cup.

*

The house was in a state of uproar when Alex got back. The police were there and had just finished questioning Mary.

'Thank God you've come!' she said, greeting Alex as though she was an old friend.

Alex told her how horrified she had been and how sorry she was. It sounded inadequate. But Mary, small and trim, seemed hardly to hear her and Alex ended by saying that she would, of course, pack her things and leave as soon as she could.

An expression of dismay crossed Mary's face. 'Oh no. Please. You must stay. I need you. I have to go into Sarlat to see the examining magistrate and there's no one here now. I can't leave Neville and I can't take him with me. I can't get him in and out of the car. Anyway, I haven't got the big car. Georges took it and no one seems to know where it is.'

It was now the turn of Alex to show dismay. Mary caught the look and said, 'It won't be for long. Just a day or two. There's someone in the village I can get but she's away until next week. Please . . . '

'Of course I will, but the only problem is someone's arrived and—'

'Oh, I know you've got your work to do. I'll be here most of the time.'

Just then a Police Inspector entered the room and told Alex he would like to ask her some questions. Mary left them, saying she would see if Neville was all right.

Alex and the Inspector had hardly sat down when a sergeant came into the house and said, 'They've found the car at Mimosa.'

The Inspector excused himself and went in search of Mary, and in a few minutes they had driven off in two police cars and Alex found herself alone in the house. She went up to Neville's room.

He looked awful. His face was like lard and his hands were trembling. He looked so vulnerable that she regretted the tough line she had taken with him.

'I'm so sorry, Neville,' she said. 'Your mother has told me how fond he was of you and how well you got on with him. I don't want to intrude, I just wanted you to know I was in the house and will be whenever your mother is out. I'll be in my room and I'll keep the door open, you can wheel yourself along if you want to.'

Then a strange thing happened. For the first time in their relationship, apart from the earlier tears, he reacted to something she had said. Slowly he began to shake his head.

'Would you like me to stay a while?'

He stretched out his hand and took hers.

'Of course,' she said. 'Of course I will.'

She sat with him for nearly an hour and all the time he clung to her hand. They watched TV. She talked to him, she read to him. By the time she heard the cars re-enter the drive her voice was hoarse and her shoulders sore. But she had a feeling of achievement rarely felt before, a sense of having broken through the protective carapace of another human being and being trusted with the vulnerable centre.

Derek Blackwood was dressed in his long black-and-white caftan and was sitting in the open window, looking down into the deep, clear waters of the mill pond. This must have been what it was like in the Castle of the Sea in the Holy Land, except that there the windows would have given out to the waters of the Mediterranean. And there was the Castle of Chillon in Switzerland, with its walls going down to the lake. And he had seen illustrations of castles in Scottish lochs with their narrow defensive windows almost touching the water.

He would have given anything to have lived then. To have had the power of life and death. To have sat at the High Table above the salt and seen the Marshal of the Hall usher in the servants with the food. To have looked out over *his* people. To have been Bohemond of Antioch! Or the Lord of Krak!

He had a plate of raw offal in front of him. Now, holding a piece in his hand, he trailed it through the water, seeing the blood form pink traceries and drift slowly down through the crystal layers of water.

He waited.

He dropped in some of the meat. One of the trout came to investigate. He was bored with trout. Then suddenly the trout veered away and he saw, in the depths, a long slender shadow.

'Come,' he said. 'Take it.'

There was a green-and-silver flash and the shadow became a pike, its long, ferox jaw thrusting out like a lance. It whirled into the meat, gulping the pieces and swinging away.

'Here,' he said and threw in a larger piece.

The pike flashed up again, jaws agape, long teeth showing, and then the meat was gone.

'One day you'll grow huge and you'll be king of the pool,' Derek said.

He moved the plate to take it to the kitchen and as he did so he noticed on the floor beside the window a small black enamel cigarette lighter. Asprey's mark was on the base. It was just as well he had found it. Wouldn't do for someone else to come across it. He remembered when Georges had first shown it to him after a trip to London. He had been envious. Georges had said he was too young for things like that. Poor Georges. The problem with him was that time had stood still. He still saw Derek and Pierre, and Neville for that matter, as children, playing children's games.

Well, Derek wasn't Peter Pan – as Georges had discovered the previous night.

18

It was a hot night and Alex and David lay naked under the open window of his bedroom in the Gardette. The river ran below them and they could just hear its faint susurration as it brushed against the retaining bank on its long curve downstream.

The three of them had had dinner on the open terrace and then Simon, still tired after the long drive south, had gone off to bed. Alex and David had had a cognac with their coffee and had then gone to David's room.

All the pent-up emotions and pressures of the past days, all the fears, all the tensions, had been blown away by the passion of their coupling and now they lay slackly in the dark, which was lit only fitfully by the point of David's cigarette as he drew on it.

She felt the sweat on her body begin to dry in the slight night breeze that blew in through the window and shivered with pleasure. It was also the pleasure of anticipation, for she knew that in an hour or so both would be ready to make love all over again.

And then she would have to go back to the Cortons' house, which was a pity.

As if reading her thoughts he said, 'Have you got a key?'

'Yes.'

He put out the cigarette and turned towards her,

rubbing his hand up and down her pliant body. 'I don't suppose Mrs Corton will get much sleep anyway, not unless she takes a pill or two.'

'She's marvellous, really. Calm. Incredibly brave. I suppose for Neville's sake. I was thinking how I'd react if—'

She stopped suddenly when she saw where that sentence was leading.

'If it was me?'

'Don't say it.'

'Look, this whole thing may just be a . . . I was going to say a figment of our imagination—'

'Thank you for the "our" but what you meant was mine.'

'I'd have thought the same if I'd been you. One needs someone to come into a situation like this and see it with fresh eyes to make sense of it.'

Irritated, she rose on an elbow and said, 'You?'

'Why not? And, from what you said, the police believe Georges' death was an accident.'

'There has to be a post-mortem but that's what it looks like to them.'

She lay back and he ran his hand over her breast and she felt again the shiver run through her body. She took his hand away and held it against her belly. 'You're distracting me. Tell me again. You only sketched it. Journalists like detail.'

So he told her again.

After Alex had left them he and Simon had driven along the river looking for one of the little *plages* and had come upon the police cars half blocking the road.

'What's happening, Dad?' Simon had said.

'I don't know.'

'Let's stop.'

'You don't want to gawp, do you?'

The hurt look on Simon's face had made him feel suddenly ashamed. He had to remember that, for all his sophistication, Simon was a boy and boys liked to see the police in action. It was better than TV. So he'd stopped the car and they had walked back.

A yellow Mercedes was parked in a small lay-by next to the river. The road rose above the river at this spot and there was a drop of about ten metres to the water.

There were half a dozen police on the road, some measuring, some photographing. A middle-aged woman, who he knew now was Mary Corton, was standing with the Inspector.

'I think I know the place,' Alex said.

'It's just the kind of place where one *would* slip. Especially in the dark.'

'But what was he doing there? That's what no one seems to know. Certainly Mary doesn't.'

'The police did say he got out of the car and fell, didn't they?'

'There were scrape marks on the rocks and on the bottoms of his shoes. But why get out there? I mean, there's nothing to see, 'specially in the dark. Unless he was meeting someone.'

'The conspiracy theory?'

'Well, you explain it then.'

'To have a pee I should have thought. Why not? It's a lay-by. The road's too narrow just to stop and get out like most Frenchmen seem to do. He was probably fastidious, anyway.'

She nodded. 'Very.'

'So he gets out, doesn't want to be seen in the headlights of approaching cars and stands between the Mercedes and the edge. But in the dark he takes that little extra step. Were they leather-soled shoes?'

'That's what I understand.' She thought of Georges' expensive Gucci loafers.

'He slips, crashes down the rockface, scraping himself, and lands in the water. Probably dead by then, or half dead anyway. And the current takes him down to Carriac and that's where he's found some hours later.'

'Quod erat demonstrandum!'

He heard the undertone of irritation and said, 'Well it's the simple explanation and the simple ones are usually best.'

'That doesn't explain the photographs, the fire, the death of the Harrises.'

'Okay, but maybe there's a perfectly good explanation for those, too.'

'And the obvious search of Petit Louis' house?'

'Thieves. Vandals, A deserted house? It's always happening.'

They made love a second time but it was not so good and Alex found herself lying in the dark feeling a sense of *tristesse* unusual for her. Perhaps it was the thought that soon she must leave and return to the Cortons' house.

'What happens next?' he said.

She knew, by the way he said it, that the question was not so much concerned with the events in Carriac but with the two of them and their lives.

'I'll finish here in three or four days.'

'And then?'

'Go back to London and write the story.'

She would be thankful to shake the dust of Carriac from her shoes, but equally she was going back to the status quo: David busy, committed to Simon, their meetings rushed affairs in a borrowed flat.

What she wanted to hear was that he loved and needed her. He usually made oblique references to marriage or living together and even though she had gently turned such statements aside they had made her feel wanted. Since their meeting that morning he had not referred to it.

'And then what?'

'Let's see what happens.'

About eleven she got dressed and went back to Carriac.

Derek held a replica of an English longbow in his hands and turned it over to look at it. He pulled on the string and let go; it hummed slightly.

'Made by peasants to be used by peasants,' he said to Pierre. 'And to think it murdered the flower of chivalry.'

Pierre had said little since his arrival an hour before. He was looking drawn and ill.

He was afraid. He felt himself afraid. It was a hot night but the sweat that ran down his chest felt cold and clammy. He had been afraid for weeks now. He had tried not to show it to Derek. He knew he was no match for him when it came to brains. All he could do was to act.

Derek fitted an arrow to the bow and drew it back. He turned and pointed the barbed steel point at Pierre.

'Don't!' Pierre said. 'Your hand might slip.'

Derek smiled, put the bow down. 'You're like an old woman. I can see you're still worried about the pictures.'

'Not if you're not.'

'Look at it logically. She's taken picture after picture since she came. It's her job. It's natural for her to show him. The receptionist told you he was a publisher, right? She's writing for a magazine. He publishes it. She shows him her pictures. Nothing could be more natural.'

Pierre shrugged. 'You asked me to watch her, to tell you everything. That's what I've done.'

'She'll go soon.'

Derek poured them both a glass of Armagnac and lit a cigarette. 'But it's not the pictures that are bothering you,' he said. 'It's Georges. Isn't it?'

Pierre stared at him without replying. He didn't want to talk about Georges. Didn't want to think about him. Because when he thought about him it made him feel physically sick. Visions of the previous night crowded back into his mind and he knew then, with a sense of despair, that there would never be a day in all his life from now on when some picture from last night would not burst into his conscious mind. Poor Georges. He had walked to his death so innocently. He remembered his screams and Derek saying, 'Save your breath, Georges. There's no one to hear you.'

And then they held him out of the window and lowered him so that his head was under water.

That had been Derek's idea. He wanted water in Georges' lungs for the post-mortem. They held him under until he drowned and then they took him to Mimosa in Derek's car, while Pierre drove the Mercedes so they wouldn't get it wet.

Derek had thought of the shoes. 'Scrape the shoes,' he had said.

Then they put them back on Georges' feet and let him slide over the edge of the road and down into the black water of the Dordogne.

When they had come back each had had two lines of coke and Pierre had felt like a giant.

That hadn't lasted. Now he said, 'You got any stuff?'

'Sure.'

Derek made a line on the back of a plate and handed it to him. It made him feel better. He knew there was something to worry about but the coke had taken the worry away.

'Feel better?'

'A lot better.'

'That's good. We must talk about Neville.'

'What about Neville?'

'Neville's the only one left who knows.'

'But he'll never talk.' He felt so good he wanted to laugh.

'You mean that literally? Georges said the psychologist thinks he will. And what then?'

'You said yourself he's implicated up to here,' he touched the top of his head.

'Listen, Neville's weak. He's always been the weakest. What if he can't hold it in and wants to confess? You know how he was always running to his mother. It was he who told her about hurting Petit Louis. And what if he trades what he knows for leniency?'

'But he swore an oath—'

'Yes, I know. But he's not like you or me. We have honour.'

19

'Do we have to, Dad?' Simon said.

'Do what?'

'You know. Go and . . . go to the other village?'

They were breakfasting on the terrace of the Gardette and already the day was hot. David knew that Simon was being diplomatic. What he meant to say was: Do we have to meet Alex?

He didn't blame him. His whole holiday had been turned on its head. He watched his son as he bit off a large piece of croissant amply covered in butter and black cherry preserve. It was like looking at a representation of himself as a child, except that Simon was wearing a T-shirt, jeans and flip-flops where he would have been wearing grey flannels, sandals and an Aertex shirt.

It would have been just his mother and himself, for his father had died when he was an infant. The statistical chances of two generations each with only one parent and one child must have been enormous and yet it had happened.

He couldn't remember his mother ever going out with another man on a serious level and he regretted it. He had often envied other boys their fathers. Was that why he so badly wanted a mother for Simon?

Yet that was only a part of it. After Susan had died he had thought he would never remarry, never find anyone to replace her. But that had changed.

He wanted more kids, three, even four. He wanted a proper family. He did not want Simon to grow up an only child with the inevitable loneliness that that meant. And he wanted a wife. No, not just a wife, he wanted Alex.

But Alex was wary. He didn't blame her. She was ambitious, wanted to get to the top. He saw it with his own staff in publishing. Women were just as ambitious as men once they'd got a start. And it was asking a hell of a lot of a young woman to take on a ready-made family, even if it was only one boy. She'd make a marvellous mother, he thought, and with her body should be able to turn out kids with the ease of an African peasant.

'What would you like to do?' he asked Simon.

'Yesterday we passed a little stream that runs down into the Dordogne. Couldn't we explore that and see if there're any pearls.'

'Pearls? There aren't any pearls in rivers.'

'There are in Scottish rivers,' Simon said with a frown. It was the kind of information that Simon tucked away. He was usually right and never liked to be contradicted. 'Someone wrote music about them. Opera, I think.'

'Of course! *The Pearl Fishers*. Bizet.'

Simon put another piece of croissant into his mouth and his dark eyes bored into David as though to say: There you are!

When they'd finished they drove the few kilometres to Carriac and David saw Alex standing in the shade of the plane-trees near the hotel, waiting for them. He drove slowly so he could look at her from a distance. She was standing with her feet slightly apart, hands on hips, the faint breeze stirring her light yellow shirt-waister, her long brown legs ending in white strappy sandals. He felt a sense of excitement and pride that she was waiting for *him*, that she was *his* woman.

At this time in the morning Carriac was humming with activity: the cranes on top of the cliff, the *gendarme*'s whistle as he let through the backed-up traffic, the crack of van der Meulen's hammer as he broke up rocks and trundled them down to the river.

It was difficult to believe that this was not its ordinary daily activity, difficult to believe that the cliff had fallen on to it, that a man's body had been found floating in the river only the day before.

When Alex heard that Simon wanted to explore she took him to the cliff and introduced him to Max Wellmann and soon the two of them were deep in the study of the cliff-face, tapping and probing and showing each other little bits of stone.

Alex and David watched them from the hotel. 'They look as though they've been doing it all their lives,' Alex said after David had ordered coffee.

David thought: I should be doing that. I should be taking Simon to explore. He felt, as he often felt, torn between wanting to be with Alex and at the same time to be with Simon. Yet why should the two be mutually incompatible?

'We never really settled anything last night,' he said.

'No.'

'I know this won't sound like I'm making much sense, specially after we came this long way to be with you, but if you want to call it off . . . I know you weren't happy about things in London and I sensed that this job was something more . . . a way of allowing you to be by yourself and think things over.'

She wanted to shake him. He was being reasonable again. Seeing her point of view. Yet wasn't that one of the things she loved about him: his generosity of spirit and the fact that he had a gentleness to go with the toughness for which his job called?

There were times she wanted to shout at him not to be reasonable; when she wanted him to pick her up and carry her off like some Visigoth. Then all their minds would be made up.

'You're right,' she said. 'I did want to think things over. But I haven't had time. From the moment I arrived I feel I've been rushing headlong into I don't know what. It's like a dream. You run down a corridor towards a door but every time you reach out to open it, it recedes.'

'It's Simon, isn't it?'

She paused for a moment then said, 'I don't think Simon likes me.'

He opened his mouth to protest but she said quickly, 'Oh I know you tell me he does, but when he looks at me I—'

'He looks at everyone that way. Even me.'

'There's always Susan. She's like a shadow. I can see him comparing. And of course I don't compare, how could I?'

'No one said it'd be easy. But as long as you and I love each other it can be made to work. These things take time. But I want you to want it. That's why I asked if you wanted to break it off for a while. Give yourself a chance to think.'

She laughed without humour. 'That's what I was supposed to be doing here.'

Simon was covered in dust and sweating when he came back. David ordered him an Orangina and he drank it without drawing breath.

Alex said, 'I have to go back to Petit Louis' cottage. I've got to take some pictures there.'

The way she said it David knew she did not want to go alone.

'Simon and I were going to one of the smaller

streams,' he said, 'but we'll come with you first. Okay, Simon?'

The eyes switched from Alex to David. They were saying one thing, while his voice said, 'Okay.'

Neville held the great two-handled sword and bent his head towards it so that his forehead touched the blade. He was feverish in the morning heat and the blade felt cool against his skin.

He had not slept. His mind had been going over and over the events of the day before.

Georges was dead.

It had taken Neville a long time to get used to his step-father. A long time to get over the jealousy he had felt when he had come calling on his mother. The one truly happy time of Neville's life was when his real father had left and he and his mother had only each other. She had lived for him then. Nothing had been too good for him: toys, food, holidays.

That's when she had begun to write for extra money. She was only a secretary in those days and secretaries in law offices were not paid much.

She had written at night. Little stories. She would sit in the living-room of their flat on the outskirts of Brighton and write at a small table while Neville watched TV.

'This is what Dickens used to do,' she said. 'He would sit in the drawing-room while guests were there and he would write and talk and listen, all at the same time.'

She had always been well-read, he thought. He had known of Dickens later at school, just as he had been taught about Jane Austen and George Eliot. His mother had actually read them for pleasure.

And then Georges had come into their lives and nothing had ever been the same again. He had hated him then. Hated him touching his mother. He had been sick for three weeks after they were married.

But slowly he had got used to Georges. He didn't beat him or his mother as his real father had done and that was something.

And after a while Georges was no longer a threat. He started on his affairs with other women and moved out of his wife's bedroom. Neville could see that his mother was treating him with disdain. It made him feel better towards Georges so that when he began to tell them about chivalry Neville had been as fascinated and eager as Derek or Pierre.

And now Georges was dead.

In spite of his feverishness, he shivered. They said he had died by accident. Had slipped on the roadside and fallen into the river.

But that was unlike Georges. He knew the area so well. He knew exactly where danger would lie. He was particular, fussy, precise.

And why was he there at all?

He knew what they thought. That he had left the car to relieve himself. But he was only ten minutes away from home and Neville was certain that Georges would have waited.

So... if it wasn't that, what was it?

And that's what frightened him.

Was it part of the pattern? Part of the road he had taken so long ago. He had started along it as a child when, as the Count of Dammartin, he had ridden into battle to save the honour of France. But what had shoplifting or beating up socialists to do with the honour of France? At the time Derek had made him believe it had everything to do with it.

And then... and then that road had inevitably brought them to the Harris house.

'They're foreigners, usurpers, maggots feeding on the living body of France,' Derek had said. 'They do nothing, create nothing, occupy space.'

But the same could be said of them all. They did nothing. They occupied space. Yet they were not going to burn down each other's houses.

He was crying now, his tears running down the blade of the sword. They hadn't meant to harm the Harrises!

That was the whole point: they were going to burn down the house while the Harrises were still in England. May was the time they came down every year. So they had decided to burn the house in April. How were they to *know*?

Neville felt all his muscles jerking and trembling as the flames of that night lit up his brain. Even as Pierre had lifted the gas cylinder and thrown it into the burning room, he had had no idea the house was occupied.

Then, dear God, he had seen the thing at the window.

He remembered that. It was etched with acid on his brain. And he remembered Derek standing back, long overcoat draped from his shoulders, the cigarette in the onyx holder. His expression was emotionless, calm, as though he was watching a field of stubble being put to the torch.

And now Georges.

Georges knew, of course. That was why. Or if he wasn't certain then he had guessed. Not about the Harris house. He didn't really care about that. No, he must have guessed about Petit Louis.

And so . . . so Derek and Pierre had killed him and somehow made it look like an accident.

And if they had killed Georges, then why not himself? He knew as much as anyone.

But would they trust him?

And if they trusted him why had they never come to see him?

He moved the wheelchair forward and closed the shutters, making sure they were locked from within.

20

Alex drove to Petit Louis' cottage in her car and David and Simon in theirs because they were going straight to the river.

It was a heavy, hot day, with clouds piling up from the south-west and Alex found herself clammy in the high humidity.

She led the way through lush, almost over-ripe countryside, and finally came to the small road that cut down towards the river.

She was driving with the windows open to get all the air she could and she was still some distance away when she smelled smoke. Her first reaction was that it was the lingering smell of the Harris house, but then she saw the fire-engine of the *sapeurs-pompiers* outside the cottage.

She got out. The cottage no longer existed. It was a mass of burnt beams, collapsed walls and corrugated iron. The firemen were packing up.

'What happened?' she asked one.

His face was grimy and he was drenched in sweat. He took off his helmet and wiped his forehead. 'Tramps, squatters, gypsies. Who knows?' He went past her to take off his heavy clothing. She followed him. David and Simon joined her.

'When did it happen?' she asked.

'Early this morning. We got a call about an hour ago. By that time it looked like this.'

He pulled off his boots and climbed into the cab. The others clambered on and the appliance drove off.

The three moved round the cottage and David said, 'What does he think happened?'

'Tramps or squatters.'

'I suppose it could have been faulty wiring.'

The hen-house was burnt and so was the lorry. Neither was closer than forty metres to the house.

Alex said, 'How would the lorry have been burnt? And the hen-house if it was faulty wiring?'

'Flames can jump gaps,' David said. 'I've seen bush fires in Australia.'

'Only if there's wind,' Simon cut in. 'And there wasn't any last night.'

Alex said to David, 'You don't want to believe, do you?'

'And you want to believe too much. If the firemen say squatters or tramps, I believe squatters or tramps. Most fires I've ever read about seem to have been started by faulty wiring. So I like to believe that, too. I'd like to believe it *wasn't* set alight deliberately.'

'Then you'll have to believe that the flames jumped from here to there!' She pointed to the hen-house.

'All right,' David said. 'Perhaps not flames, but sparks.'

'Would sparks have set fire to the lorry?'

David was becoming irritated. 'I don't know. Why not?'

Simon said, in a knowing voice, 'Not unless they landed in the petrol tank. And then it would have exploded.'

'Christ Almighty!' David turned to Alex. 'Listen, sweetie, you've got to watch this conspiracy theory.'

She felt her own irritation level shoot up. 'Oh?'

'You came down here at a bad time for Carriac. The people thought they'd just got rid of the media, just got everything quietened down. Then you arrive and start turning over stones to see what's underneath. *Of course* they're going to treat you as though you are some kind of pariah. And *of course* you're going to become incensed and suspicious.'

'David, I—'

'And this doctor. You know nothing about him. But he tells you some story and implants suspicion in your mind. And once that happens *everything* is suspicious.'

'You saw the pictures!' she said. 'You saw the arms at the window!'

'All I saw was a picture of a burning house. What you say are arms could have been branches of a tree, anything...'

He was suddenly aware of her expression and he said, 'Darling, I'm sorry. Look, why don't you take the day off? Why don't we all go for a swim? Lie in the sun. Have a nice expensive lunch at one of the hotels and just forget things for a while.'

She was about to say something crushing when she thought: *Be a good girl. Don't have a row. Don't spoil things. Remember what it was like when he wasn't here.*

'Okay, we'll go for a swim. Where?'

Simon described his stream. 'I know it,' she said. 'It comes down near St Cybranet. I'm going to take a few more pictures round here and then I'll go back and pick up my swimsuit. You go on and I'll meet you there.'

She watched the car go off down the road and suddenly felt alone and vulnerable. She shot half a roll of film and got back into her car and felt safer. Whatever or whoever had started the fire, one thing was certain: if Petit Louis had taken any other pictures they were all gone now.

She drove back to Carriac and the Cortons' house.

On the way she began to feel guilty, for she had not seen Mary that morning to check if she would need her at any point during the day.

The problem was that the events of the last few days were turning over and over in her mind, occupying it to the exclusion of almost everything else.

She had spoken lightly of the play within the play, but it was becoming more of a reality, or at least that's what she thought. If David was right then everything was her imagination. But she couldn't believe that.

She went quietly into the house because she did not want to spend time with Neville. She looked in at the door of his room and saw that it was in semi-darkness. She could just make out his silhouette against the shutters. He had the sword in his hands but was sitting quite still, as though deep in thought. She supposed she should go in and be friendly but she wanted to be with David.

She tiptoed along to her own room. She thought she heard a voice coming from Mary's turret but she didn't want to see her either.

Quietly she got her swimsuit and a towel and was in her bathroom when she heard not one but two voices in the corridor outside her room. She stood silently as they passed and then, ashamed of herself, she went out to offer to stay with Neville. She stopped at the top of the stairs. Below her, in the hall, she saw Mary and Max Wellmann. Their arms were round each other and they were kissing passionately.

Alex shrank against the wall and then slipped back to her own room.

A few minutes later there was a knock on her door and Mary came in. 'I saw your car,' she said. 'I didn't know you were in.'

'I've just come to get a swimsuit.'

'It is hot, isn't it? Where are you swimming?'

'My friends have gone up to the stream near St Cybranet.'

'It's lovely up there.'

Alex could see no trace of passion or guilt on her face or in her eyes. It was hard to believe that her husband had been found dead so recently.

'I was hoping you could be in this evening,' Mary said. 'Say, from about eight. And bring your friends to keep you company. I won't be late.'

Alex paused for a fraction of a second. Had she misjudged this woman? Was there something deeper here than she thought? Was she . . . Stop it! For God's sake stop it!

'Of course,' she said. 'I'll be glad to.'

She drove along the Dordogne, crossed to the south bank, and continued towards St Cybranet. A beautiful clear stream ran down the valley. At some places it was only a few yards from the road, at others half a kilometre.

She looked across the rich meadows for David's car. After a few minutes her eye was caught by a movement. Someone was running across the fields towards the road. There was something about the figure that caused her to slam on the brakes. As it drew nearer she saw it was Simon and she felt the lower part of her stomach clench in apprehension.

'It's Dad!' he shouted as he reached the car. 'He's hurt!'

'Get in.'

She took a track across the meadow, bucking and bumping, and soon came to the line of trees which marked the stream and saw David's car.

Simon ran ahead of her and they came to a beautiful long pool at the bottom of a rocky chute. It was one of those idyllic places seen sometimes in holiday brochures. It was about thirty metres long, with a sandy bottom. The river poured down into it, frothing over medium-sized brown stones. One side was fringed by a grassy bank, the other by trees and brush.

David, in his swimming costume, was lying on the bank. As they came down towards him he moved. He gave a groan and held his head as he slowly sat up. Blood was pouring down one side of his face from a cut beneath his hair.

'Are you all right?' Her voice was frightened, shrill.

'I don't know.'

'What happened?'

'God knows.'

He seemed dazed and confused.

Simon said, 'I'd gone exploring. I wanted to see if there were any freshwater crayfish or mussels and when I came back Dad was half in and half out of the water.'

He showed her marks in the sandy fringe. 'I managed to pull him up here. But he was unconscious. I knew you were coming so I ran towards the road.'

'What do you think happened?' It was addressed more to Simon than to David.

He pointed to the stones over which the water was bubbling. 'They're slippery. They've got algae on them. If Dad had tried to cross he may have slipped.'

She wet her towel and used it to wipe some of the blood off David's face. His eyes were dull and he kept blinking as though to clear his head.

'We must get him to a hospital,' she said. 'We'll take your car.'

David had a big blue Volvo estate and they managed to lie him down in the back. Alex drove them into Sarlat.

On her visits there she had seen a hospital sign at the bottom of the main street. She turned left up the slight hill. When she reached it she found it was not a general hospital as she had imagined but the Clinique les Pins.

Between them, each taking an arm, they managed to get David to walk into Casualty. A nurse in a nun's habit helped him on to an examining couch, then she showed them to a waiting-room.

They waited for more than an hour. Alex was impressed by Simon's courage. He had not cried and had not become emotionally upset.

'He's going to be all right,' she said.

'I know.'

A young doctor came in. He could not have been more than Alex's age but looked even younger because his hair was crew cut.

'Can you tell me 'ow it 'appen?' he said in English.

'As far as we know he was swimming and slipped on rocks.'

He nodded as though this explanation was satisfactory. 'He 'as a concussion. He must stay in tonight and maybe tomorrow. It is for observation.'

'I understand.'

'Please do not mistake me. But this is a private clinic. Do you know if he 'as insurance?'

Simon said, 'He got it for both of us, and the car. Everything.'

They looked through David's clothes but his wallet was missing. The doctor watched impassively. Alex said, 'If Simon says they have insurance then they have. His wallet may be where they were swimming or at the hotel. But it makes no difference. If there's any problem I'll pay.'

'That is all right, then. You can see him in the morning.'

'He can't remember what happened,' Simon said.

'It is often like that with concussion. He will be okay.' Simon looked relieved.

They left David's Volvo in the hospital parking area and took a taxi to St Cybranet so that Alex could pick up her car.

They searched the area around the pool but there was no sign of the wallet.

'We'll come back tomorrow,' Alex said. 'It's too late now.'

'Are you coming to the hotel? You can have Dad's room.'

For the first time she heard a slight tremor in his voice.

'That's what we've got to talk about.' She put out a hand, much as his mother might, as though it was the most natural thing in the world. 'Come on. Let's get away from here.'

He took her hand and they walked quickly to the car.

'Visa. American Express. National Westminster Bank. Eurocheque.' Derek spread the cards out in a fan. He and Pierre were having a drink on the terrace outside the mill. It was built overlooking the mill pond and the water was rushing down the flume.

He opened another part of the wallet and pulled out several receipts. He looked at one. 'Insurance,' he said.

There was a pile of francs on the table. He pushed them towards Pierre. 'Buy something for the bike.'

Then he tossed everything over the balustrade into the foaming water.

'When he wakes up he'll have nothing except his passport.' Pierre said.

'That's what we want. Someone who isn't going to stay.'

'Have you got any stuff?'

'Later. We're going to need it then.'

Even though the evening was hot, Pierre felt his skin go cold.

21

It had been a long day for Neville. His mother had been in several times to sit with him and she had spoken about Georges. He wished he could ask questions but that wasn't possible. For the remainder of the time he had been thinking and remembering. And the sword was always near at hand.

Now, at dusk, it was the centre of his world, replacing the electronic game. It was the sword that Sire de Charny had used at Poitiers. And *he* was Sire de Charny – to hell with Derek.

It was strange that Georges had given it to him. Was it a bribe? What had he said: One day you will speak? One day you will tell the truth? Something like that.

The words had been obscure. He remembered wondering at the time what he meant. Georges sometimes spoke like that. But the more he thought about it the less they made sense.

All day he had been asking himself questions: What was it that Georges had seen? Had he seen everything? And why had he been there when it happened?

They were questions he had never allowed to enter his mind before because he had simply assumed that any question to be asked would be asked of him, Neville. And as long as he could not speak he could not answer.

But now that Georges was dead Neville allowed

his mind to bring back pictures he had rigorously excluded. And suddenly he had seen that he might have been putting a wrong interpretation on Georges' words.

What if they had been a threat? If that was so then it meant that he, Georges, didn't want Neville to speak the truth.

Could that be right?

Of course he hadn't made it clear. It was fuzzy.

That was probably deliberate for neither Georges nor anyone else knew when Neville would suddenly get back the use of his voice.

But what was Georges afraid of once Neville did? That's what he had been pondering all day.

And he had come up with an answer. Maybe not *the* answer but an answer.

Questions.

He was afraid that Neville might ask questions.

It was this that had finally precipitated itself out of Neville's mind. And the reason it had taken so long was a matter of guilt: when you are overwhelmed by your own guilt you don't recognise it in others.

Neville had always assumed the questions would be aimed at *him*.

This inversion – such a simple inversion – was like so many things in Neville's short life that had turned out precisely the opposite of what they had at first seemed.

He remembered once being beaten by his real father for mistaking a gesture. Neville, on his way to play with a neighbour, had thought his father was waving goodbye when in fact he was beckoning. Neville had waved quickly in reply, turned and hurried on. When he came home an hour or so later his father was white with rage.

He pressed the cool blade of the sword against his face. Which might mean that Georges had never seen Petit Louis there at all. Or at least not when... not when they...

He felt again as though his brain was on fire, except that everything that had happened to Petit Louis was much worse than the Harris house. That had been a mistake. A tragic error. And you couldn't be wholly blamed for a mistake.

But Petit Louis was different. There had been no mistake there.

You could say he had brought it on himself. From the moment he had taken the pictures of the Harris house in flames he had sealed his own fate. If it had only been Pierre or Neville things would have been different. But you didn't threaten Derek. Not ever.

Of course he could understand the justice in it from Petit Louis' point of view. The burn scars on his legs would never go away. And the Harris house was another burning.

You don't make much money from selling wood.

Those had been his exact words when he had shown them the colour prints. They had only seen four but four was enough.

Derek knew all about colour film. This was Kodachrome 64. When it was processed you got transparencies but you could always have colour prints made as well. So Petit Louis had put the transparencies up for sale. One million francs. It wasn't much, he said, between the three of them. Not to avoid prison.

They had agreed to his price. He had given them a week to pay.

Of course Derek never had any intention of paying. They had watched Petit Louis. They had waited. One night when he was out they had gone to the cottage and turned it upside down, but they'd found nothing.

Then, on their way back to Derek's mill, they had been lucky, they'd seen his lorry parked on the outskirts of Carriac. They'd stopped a kilometre away and crept back into the village. Derek carried a reproduction of a twelfth century mace, a wooden club with an iron-shod head.

Petit Louis had seen them. He'd started to run. But Pierre had caught him easily. And there in the dark alley Derek had sentenced him to death and struck him with the mace.

Petit Louis had dropped to his knees. Derek had handed the mace to Pierre.

'Now, you. Then Neville. Then we'll park the lorry at Mimosa and throw him into the river.'

And Pierre had struck and Petit Louis had given a dreadful groan and fallen on to his side. And Derek had taken the mace and offered it to Neville.

And Neville had said, 'For God's sake no! I can't.'

'You can! You yellow bastard!'

And then the cliff had come down.

'It's going to be a hot night,' Alex said. 'Are you sure you want a blanket as well?'

'Yes,' Simon said.

They were in the second spare room in the Corton house, just along the corridor from Alex's.

When Mary had heard what had happened to David she had, at first, told Alex she must not think of staying in the house but take Simon to a hotel in Sarlat if that's what they wanted to do. But Alex had pointed out there was nothing they could do for David and if there was a spare bed Simon could sleep in the house.

And that's how it had been arranged. Alex and Simon had had dinner at the hotel and had come back to the house and Mary had gone off to... wherever it was she was going.

'Do you like it tucked in?' Alex said.

'Yes.' His voice was subdued.

'You can always untuck it if you get hot.'

It was the kind of conversation she had not had for years, not since she had been a little girl making up her bed with her mother.

In London this scene would have been impossible; here, under the circumstances, it seemed the most natural thing in the world.

He had borne up marvellously throughout the period at the hospital, she thought, but once they returned to the river to look for David's wallet, he seemed to shrink from a semi-adult, with a great deal of confidence, to a little boy without much at all.

She remembered how relieved he had looked when she had suggested to Mary that he stay at the house.

'I'll have to look in on Neville,' she said. 'Do you want to meet him?'

'Do I have to?'

'Well, perhaps not tonight. But I think it would be nice for him if you said hello tomorrow.'

Suddenly she heard her own mother's voice: 'Alex, darling, I want you to...'

That was being a mum, too, she thought. But the wrong sort.

'Let's go and phone the hospital,' she said.

Neville had watched Alex and Simon come up the drive through the slats of the shutters. His mother had explained why the boy was coming; something about an accident to his father. He was jealous of the boy. And of the father. He had liked Alex, liked holding her hand. At any other time... he had let the fantasies unroll in his head like a movie. Only he wasn't sure what Sire de Charny would have done. Made up poetry or songs? Was there much sexual activity at that time between knights and their ladies? Derek said there was, but Derek thought he knew everything.

Yellow bastard!

Or a hero. That's what the newspapers and the media had said. A hero.

Sometimes he even believed it. But at other times the pictures were there in his mind: the crashing of the rocks, the dust, the cries of the injured.

He had no idea what had happened. For one horrifying split second he thought it was God's punishment for what they had done to Petit Louis, then he realised it was an avalanche of a sort. He couldn't move. His legs were pinned. He shouted and shouted but no one came.

His mouth was full of grit and so were his eyes and hair. Otherwise he was uninjured. It was just that he couldn't move his legs.

And then, over the rubble had come this thing, this legless alligator. It pulled itself along on its elbows. The side of its face was pulped where Pierre had struck. An eye was missing. But in its hands it held a rock about half the size of a football and Neville knew exactly what was going to happen. Petit Louis was going to pull himself along until he reached Neville and then he was going to lift the rock and smash it down on his head.

He yelled. Petit Louis began the process of pulling himself up on to his knees. He was scowling at Neville through his one remaining eye. His top lip had vanished and the stumps of his teeth were covered in blood and dirt. He raised the rock to bring it down on Neville's head. And then, as though an electric charge had passed through his body, he gave a series of jerks and fell forward, his face touching Neville's arm.

And that's how Georges found them. Petit Louis was dead. Neville was hysterical.

'What were you doing here?' Georges asked him, his face contorted.

'I didn't want him to die,' Neville said, tears and mucus flowing down his face.

'What were you looking for?'

But Neville repeated his sentence over and over. 'I didn't want him to die!'

When others heard it they said to each other: *He didn't want him to die so he tried to save him.*

By the time Mary arrived the story was set like concrete. Neville had tried to save Petit Louis. Neville was a hero. And also by that time Neville could not – or would not – speak.

But now, because Georges was dead and Neville had allowed the pictures back into his mind, he heard Georges' voice again.

What were you doing here?

Was that the question you asked an injured victim?

Yes, if you had seen what the victim thought you had seen.

What were you looking for?

It didn't make sense. If Georges had seen the killing of Petit Louis then he knew that Neville had not been looking for anything.

He tried to remember exactly where Petit Louis had been when they had crept back into the dark village. He had been in the alleyway beyond the Dutchman's house, crouched against the base of the cliff where the house joined it.

Pierre had chased him into the next alleyway and that's where they had finished him.

Now, Neville realised that the questions Georges had asked him were really questions that should have been asked of Georges. *What were you doing there, Georges? What were you looking for?*

His fingers ran down the sword blade, feeling the sharp edge.

And now Georges was dead and he heard again in his head Derek's words: *Then we'll park the lorry at Mimosa and throw him in the river.*

And his mother's words: *Georges parked the car at Mimosa. You know, darling, where the lay-by is. And he must have slipped and fallen . . .*

What would Sire de Charny do now?

22

Alex and Simon were in Georges' study. Alex was phoning the hospital in Sarlat and Simon was looking around the walls at the armour and the books and the weapons of war.

'Thank you . . . yes. Yes. I understand. All right . . . '

She put the phone down and turned to Simon. 'As far as they can tell there's nothing wrong with your father. He's asleep. We'll pick him up in the morning. That's lovely, isn't it?'

Simon nodded. 'I knew Dad would be all right.' But his eyes were still uneasy.

He glanced past her and pointed to the fork-tongued banner on the wall behind the desk. 'That's a battle flag,' he said. 'Orangefire. A name like that.'

'It's called the oriflamme,' she said.

'And that's the battle cry.' He pointed to the words, MONTJOIE – ST DENIS!

Just then she heard a noise at the rear of the house. She switched off the study light, thinking that Mary was coming back.

She heard two voices. Max Wellmann? Were Mary and Max coming back to the house? She could hardly believe it.

The voices stopped but over the distant thud of the music coming from Neville's room she heard a door open and close. Then another. And a third. It was as though someone was searching the ground-floor rooms.

All the strains and uncertainties of the past days coalesced. She put a finger to her mouth and softly they went round behind Georges' desk. Then she pulled him down with her. In the dark she could feel rather than see the bewilderment in his eyes.

The light was suddenly switched on for a few seconds and then switched off again. From her position she could see nothing.

She heard footsteps leaving the doorway and indicated to Simon to stay where he was. She went to the door and put her eye to the crack at the hinge. The hall was lit and she saw the shadow of a man moving up the stairs. He reached the landing and walked along towards Neville's room. The light behind him threw his shadow on to the white wall in stark chiaroscuro.

Fear, true fear, the kind she had experienced when she lay in the lorry at Petit Louis' cottage, gripped her and she felt a sense of panic. The man became visible. It was Derek.

And then she thought: Don't be silly! Derek was Neville's friend. So was Pierre. They were coming to see him at last.

But even so the fear did not leave her.

She took Simon by the hand and led him swiftly across the downstairs hall, opened the front door and said, 'I want you to wait here for me.'

She told herself again that Derek and Pierre were friends of Neville but somehow it didn't make her feel any better.

What she wanted to do was put Simon in her car, drive to Sarlat, put up at a hotel for the night, pick up David the following morning – and get the hell away from the Dordogne.

But Mrs Corton had trusted her.

She went back into the house and swiftly mounted the

stairs. There was no sound of music now, only the soft murmur of voices. She told herself it would do Neville good to see them.

She reached the door of his room. Pierre was on his knees in front of Neville's secret cupboard. He was trying to force it. Neville's wheelchair was empty and the window in front of it open. Derek was standing on the other side of the room, his back to the door. He was bareheaded and wearing his white suit. He was smoking, the holder gripped between his teeth. A table lamp threw his shadow against the wall.

She had opened her mouth to say good evening when suddenly her heart froze. Seeing the shadow changed everything. She was looking again at the transparencies. It was like one of those old-fashioned puzzles where one drawing is hidden inside another. Once you see part of it the whole suddenly becomes clear. The silhouette in the photographs was Derek's. The twig coming from the side of his head was the cigarette holder.

He turned, hearing her, and she blurted out. 'You! The Harris house!'

Derek and Pierre had each had two lines of coke before leaving the mill-house. Derek was feeling tremendous. He smiled widely at her.

'And a very good evening to you, Miss Bridgman,' he said and raised the pistol he held in his right hand. *'Bonne chance!'*

He fired. But she was already moving. The bullet whacked into the wall behind her.

She was running.

She fled along the corridor and down the staircase, jumping two and three stairs at a time. She heard a commotion on the top landing but did not look round. She heard the thudding of feet. She heard, as though in the distance, the snapping noise of the pistol but had no idea where the bullet had gone.

She found herself outside. Simon was standing against the wall of the porch. 'Come!' she said, gripping his hand.

He had the sense not to question her, but ran at her side. They made for the car. It was standing in the drive in full view. She heard the front door open and knew that if they crossed the open driveway they would make excellent targets. Instead she veered away to her right, entering the shrubberies and making for the darkest part of the garden.

She stopped once and heard running footsteps on the hard gravel. Her heart was pounding in her ears and her breath was ragged. Obliterating the picture of Derek's silhouette was another picture, even more frightful. It was the empty wheelchair. The open window. The helpless young man flung down on to the hard earth below.

But why? Why had they killed Neville?

She heard someone brush through leaves thirty or forty metres away.

'What do they want?' Simon whispered.

'To harm us.'

She had no real plan in her mind. Her first thoughts had been to get away from Derek and Pierre. For the moment she had achieved that. What now?

She squatted down next to Simon and said softly, 'Listen to me. There are two men in the grounds looking for us. I know something about them. Something bad. And because you're with me they may think you know as well. So we've got to get out. There's no use running for the gate. They'll be watching that. Same with the car. So we'll have to go down to the river. We can walk and wade a bit and get up to the village. And then I can use the phone at the hotel and call the police.'

Then she had to find Mary and warn her and tell her what she thought may have happened and what might be lying on the ground underneath Neville's open window.

That was the last thing in the world she wanted to do! But she couldn't let Mary go back to the house and discover it all for herself.

In the velvety dark she could just make out Simon's thin white face. They were pointed at her like twin gun barrels. His presence doubled her own fear. What if things went wrong? He must be confused and terrified. And that would add to her problem. What if she couldn't get him to safety? She thought of David lying in hospital and she felt something inside her cringe.

'Do you understand what I'm saying, darling?'

'Of course,' he said. She heard the trace of contempt, the patronising tone. It was the old Simon, and she felt a flood of relief.

'Come on, then.'

The garden sloped down to the river's edge. They made their way through shrubberies and across the lawn and finally came to the dense brush by the river's edge. It was almost impenetrable, a mass of close-growing wild willow and poplar saplings. Mosquitos rose in clouds from pools of trapped, stagnant water.

They were not so much on a bank but part of the river bed itself. It would be under water at times of heavy rain but at the moment it was a mixture of round stones, sand, roots, bush, puddles, long pieces of rusty wire, and driftwood.

The moment they entered this bush they were engulfed. Much of the foliage was more than head high, and within a few moments Alex was sweating profusely and the mosquitos were settling on her, making her want to flail her arms and run.

They were on the north bank and Carriac was about four hundred metres on their left. It might have been four hundred miles. They could see no lights and the only sounds that penetrated this jungle were the faint lapping of the river and the high-pitched whine of the mosquitos.

She tried to be silent but she could hardly see where she was going and her leather-soled shoes scraped on the rock. Simon was wearing trainers and was sure-footed.

Branches whipped at her and thorns pulled at her blouse. Every few yards they stopped and listened. They heard no noises of pursuit. She bent to Simon's ear and said, 'Are you all right?'

'Yes.'

They went on, walking a few yards, then listening. Walking, listening. Then suddenly Alex fell.

She did not see the hole. Her right foot went down into it and she fell forward, wrenching her knee. She tried to stifle a cry but the pain was intense.

Simon helped her on to her feet but she could not place her weight on her right leg. She felt tears of pain and anger at the back of her eyes.

'Are *you* all right?' Simon said in his turn.

What would be the point of telling him how she really felt?

'Yes.'

She tried to take a step but once her weight transferred to her right leg the pain shot through her knee on white-hot wires and she cried out again.

'I'll help you,' Simon said.

She put her right arm round his shoulders and they went forward.

Her cry had been heard.

When Derek and Pierre had lost them in the garden, Pierre had gone down into the bush on the side of the river and he had begun to work his way downstream. Now he stopped and turned, and like a fox-hound that has rediscovered the scent, he began to retrace his steps.

Derek also heard the cry. He had been watching the car and the gate and then had moved on to the road and was above Alex and Simon.

He had thought he'd heard movement but could not be sure against the noises of the river itself. Now he checked the safety catch on the pistol and then went back along the road and called to Pierre.

'I know,' Pierre called back. 'I heard.'

Derek made his way back along the road and stopped just short of the hotel. He knew the river like the back of his hand. The part of the bed on which the woman and the boy were trying to escape gradually grew narrower and petered out as it reached the village. For the river came down on to the village and made its turn there, and all along the retaining wall the water was turbulent.

They would simply run out of dry land and would have to get into the water, and Derek did not give much for their chances then, for the river was alive with boils and whirlpools as it swung away from the wall. Or they would have to turn back towards Pierre.

'There's someone behind us,' Simon whispered.

'I know. I heard him call.'

They went on. Alex was in an enclosed world of pain. Each step was torture. She wanted to sit. To lie. To be anything but upright.

'It's getting narrower,' Simon said.

A sheer bank loomed on their left now and the water was only a few yards away on their right.

'There's an iron ladder fixed to the wall farther on, near the hotel.'

They had come to the end of the manageable part

of the river bed and were on a small sand pit. Ahead of them was the dark, spooling water.

'But won't one of them be waiting at the ladder?' Simon said.

In her pain she had not thought of the obvious. She could visualise Derek, in his arrogant way, waiting for them to try and expend their energy by swimming against the current. And then . . . She tried not to think of what would happen then.

They were trapped by the water in front and by Pierre behind. Their only escape was the bank to their left. But it was sheer.

'Try further on,' she said.

They entered the water. The current dragged at them.

Simon, who was leading, said, 'Hold on to these.' There was grass and roots and small shrubs along the bank. They caught them and pulled themselves along.

He said, 'I can feel the bottom.' He stood up. The water came only to his knees. He was standing on the pile of rock emptied into the river by van der Meulen.

Alex remembered how Thomas and the *gendarme* had pulled Georges' body up; how they had cut steps in the bank.

She was holding on to a trailing plant. The current was dragging her, weakening her hold. She told Simon where to look.

He slowly waded across the pile of rock and touched the damp earth of the bank.

'I've found it.'

She struggled through the water until she was on her good leg on the rocks. Simon was holding out a hand. She caught it and pulled herself to the bank.

They climbed up on steps that resembled those cut

in an ice slope. As she placed the weight on her right leg she thought she was going to faint.

Simon reached the top of the bank. He held on to a sapling with one hand and offered her the other. Without it she would have fallen back into the water and been swept away.

They were up on the road and back in the world. In the distance was a street light near the hotel and she could see a figure standing on the *quai* near the iron ladder. Derek. Somehow they had to get past him to the hotel and the telephone.

She told Simon and he said, 'When I went to help Dr Wellmann I saw a path along the bottom of the cliff. Maybe that'll take us to the back of the hotel.'

'Let's try.'

They had to cross the road before they could enter the alleys and broken houses. She couldn't tell whether Derek was looking at the river or not, but they had to take a chance. With her arm round Simon's shoulders and his round her waist, they hobbled across the dead ground.

Once they entered the rubble area they were cut off from the village lights. The alleys running between the river and the base of the cliff were cleared early on.

These alleys were not more than fifty or sixty metres long and Alex hurried as fast as her leg would allow. They reached the top of the alley and the cliff loomed above them.

'This way,' Simon said.

There was a narrow ledge running along the base of the cliff. They had to pull themselves up on to it.

Simon said, 'It's not very wide.'

As they moved along it towards the hotel they brushed the cliff with their left shoulders and to their right were the piles of rubble, some still four and five metres high.

They picked their way along this shelf until they came to the next alley and the next. The hotel was less than a hundred metres away.

When they reached the area above van der Meulen's house they paused for a moment and Derek said, '*Bon soir.* Nice to see you again.'

He was standing below them near what had once been van der Meulen's front door. There was enough light to see his face and he was wearing the same wide smile he had worn in Neville's bedroom.

Alex swung round, looking for an avenue of escape. Her leg gave way underneath her. She fell back against the cliff. Stones clattered past her. She reached for one to throw at Derek, but it was all too late.

She saw everything in slow motion.

Simon was bending to help her.

Derek was raising the gun.

At that moment, like some medieval fetch, a figure rose from the rockpile between them. He was holding a sword in his hands and now he raised it above his head.

'*Montjoie!*' he cried. '*St Denis!*'

And he swung the great two-handed sword in a glittering downward arc.

Derek had turned at the same time and fired. But it was too late to stop the flow of action which Neville had started.

The sword bit into the left-hand side of Derek's neck, severing the muscles, the veins and arteries, and cutting deep into the shoulder bone.

For a moment he stood, with the sword still in him, unable to believe what had happened. Then slowly his knees bent and he fell forward.

Neville was leaning against the rubble pile, holding his throat.

Alex could see Pierre standing at the bottom of the alley. He turned and ran.

Simon was bending over her. 'Are you all right?' he said anxiously.

'Yes, I'm all right.'

Slowly she put down the rock that had been meant for Derek. It clinked. She looked down at it. It was not a rock, but a camera.

23

The long summer's day was coming to an end. It was still hot but a breeze was riffling the sea and the sun was low on the horizon. It had been a different kind of summer's day from the Dordogne. Here, in Granville, on the Cotentin Peninsula, the day had been the stuff of kids' holidays: sand, bare feet, ice creams and sunburn.

Alex had been working on her article, sitting on the wide balcony of one of the strange Edwardian houses – all mansard roofs and wooden curlicues – which perch high on the cliffs above the beach.

To her left was the Hôtel les Bains and the Centre de Thalassothérapie, below her the long wide sandy beach disappearing away to her right in a jumble of rocks, then more beach and ending in the seaside villas of Donville.

They had been on their way back to London from the Dordogne when they had stopped for the night in Granville. They had arrived in dismal weather but when they awoke the following morning the sky was blue, the sun was out and the bad weather of the previous weeks was gone. They had decided to stay.

Because of the foul weather the town was deserted and they had their choice of houses for rent. They had chosen the maddest. A kind of Charles Addams house built around the turn of the century with rooms at varying angles and levels.

After what had happened in Carriac almost any place would have been heaven. Neither she nor David had been in Granville before, usually hurrying, like most other visitors to France, down the peninsula, trying to get as far south as possible on the first day of a holiday.

They were enchanted. So was Simon. There was a Museum of the Sea not too far away. There were rocks to investigate. There was the whole of Brittany to explore.

A pattern had developed. David and Simon would go off exploring, Alex would work through the day and by late afternoon would be sick of being by herself, sick of sitting at her typewriter, ready to be entertained and loved.

And that's when David and Simon would return from visiting a lighthouse in Finistère or a World War II museum in Normandy. In the evenings, Simon would often stay in and watch the English language movies on French TV while she and David would go off to have sumptuous meals of oysters and langoustes, crabs and mussels.

But in spite of the weather, the food, the house, David's loving presence, an area of darkness sat at the back of her mind. Someone had tried to kill her and she would never feel quite the same again. Something in her make-up had changed subtly. The absoluteness of her own being, its invulnerability, had been lost for ever.

To some this came with a death in the family, a loss, a divorce, treachery. To Alex it had come when she had fallen back against the cliff in Carriac and had expected her life to end in a matter of seconds.

She could still see the picture in her mind with total clarity and knew it would never go away. And 'never' was a word that frightened her, for so far in her life there had always been second and third chances. It came as a shock to realise there were circumstances when first was last and last first.

It had seemed like being suddenly flung back into the Middle Ages: the great sword gleaming in the starlight, the dreadful crunch as it bit into flesh and bone – it had almost severed Derek's arm from his body and the very shock of it had killed him in minutes.

And Neville, holding himself against the rocks, trying to staunch the blood that was spurting from the bullet wound in his neck.

Everything had happened so fast that she had no time to wonder how he had got there, or to register that he was standing, moving, and that there was nothing wrong with his speech. In her ears, all her life, would be the cry *Montjoie – St Denis!*.

She wondered how many knights and foot-soldiers had heard it at Crécy and Poitiers and at a hundred other battles – just before they died.

Like Derek.

And then, of course, had come the aftermath. The police, the investigation, questions and more questions, until finally, like a jigsaw puzzle, with each of them handing over their pieces, an Inspector from Périgueux had managed to put together a picture of what had happened.

Some parts of the puzzle would always be blank because some people were dead and their pieces had died with them. But in general the picture was understandable, and it was the best view of the series of events that had led to the deaths of Petit Louis and Georges and Derek that they were ever going to have.

After the police had left and Mary Corton had gone into Sarlat to be with Neville in hospital, Max Wellmann had said, 'We all play games when we're kids. But then we grow up. If we don't then this is what happens. Make-believe blurs into reality, actions take over from the imagination, reality itself becomes infused with dangerous additives. Life is too serious for adult games.'

Which was how the three young men reached the watershed of the Harris house. Of course they hadn't *meant* to harm the old couple. Of course they were *sorry*, or at least Neville and Pierre were sorry. But it was all a bit late.

And Petit Louis had everything on film. That's when the games had turned sour, when the chain reaction had set in.

If they'd paid up, nothing more might have been heard from him. On the other hand he might have bled them all their lives. Once the course was set, it was difficult to move to a different one. Even Neville understood that.

And once Derek had spotted Petit Louis' lorry parked near the village, once they had run back to find him, then events were unstoppable.

But why had Petit Louis been in the village at all at that time of night?

That's what had always bothered Alex, and that's where the camera had come in, the one she had picked up *in extremis* thinking it was a rock to hurl at Derek. Petit Louis must have pushed it into a hole in the rock just before he ran.

The police had taken the camera from her, had had the film in it developed and she had seen the finished pictures.

From Petit Louis' position on the path that ran along the base of the cliff he must have been level with and able to see into the top window of Thomas van der Meulen's house.

The bedroom window.

It had been a hot, close night. The windows were open, the curtains moving in the sultry wind that had presaged the storm. All he had to do was wait for the right moments.

It was like a strip cartoon. The first shot had been taken once Georges had got out of bed and switched on the light. You could see him dressing plainly enough.

Then Marie, Thomas' wife, had got up and Petit Louis had taken a shot of her naked, fleshy body.

After a few more shots of them dressing there was a picture of the front door. It was badly underexposed but Alex had been able to make out the figure of a man opening it.

Then Petit Louis had turned the telephoto back to the bedroom for the next series of shots. They showed a man, easily identified as van der Meulen, standing on the threshold.

In the next shot Georges' arms were up, as though he was both arguing and defending himself. But van der Meulen's attention was on his wife.

The following picture showed van der Meulen striking his wife with his balled fist. She was falling back towards the bed. In this shot Georges was making for the bedroom door but had half turned towards the window as though he had seen something on his way out.

That was the last of the series.

No one would ever know what happened in the next few seconds. No one would know how badly Marie van der Meulen had been injured by her husband. No one would know what Georges had seen or heard – a movement, the click of a shutter, a flash of light on the camera body, the crouched figure of Petit Louis on the cliff path? The police thought he knew what Petit Louis had been up to and that's what caused him to search the rubble piles at night. He was searching for the camera. And then the scenario of the following moments: Georges descending the stairs of the house to street level, and during those very seconds Petit Louis fleeing from the three young men.

And Georges – guilty Georges – coming out into the night *knowing* he had been seen.

And then: crash!

When David was fetched from the hospital and pitched into the midst of the crisis, he had looked at the pictures and finally said, 'What the butler saw. Updated.'

It was true, she thought. Except the butler was a wood merchant with a newly acquired taste for blackmail.

This had not emerged all at once but in bits and pieces, and the key was Neville.

Alex had sat with him several times in Sarlat hospital in the days that followed the shooting. By then he was using the pad and pencil which the police had given him with so much fluency it had become almost impossible to stop him. The pad was full of questions and statements and more questions and statements. It seemed that his long silence had produced a driving need to unburden himself of every tiny detail.

His mother was there every day and all day and Max Wellmann came with her.

She was grey-faced and looked older. But it was apparent that she and Max were in love and that she was leaning on him now like a crutch. Alex sympathised wholly with her. She could not ask her, of course, about their relationship, but from small things said she managed to put together her own picture. It was commonplace enough. For years Georges had been womanising and Mary had started an affair with Max as a *quid pro quo* – and then they had fallen in love. But there was one big snag: Mary was a Catholic and so was Max. There was no question of her divorcing Georges.

Now Mary was filled with guilt about Neville. She was blaming herself for going out to dinner with Max that night. But what, Alex had wanted to know, could she have done even if she had stayed?

Got herself killed, too, Max had said.

In any case, as Alex knew only too well, Neville hadn't been in the house.

The moment he had worked out that Georges had been in the village earlier than he had said, he knew that his vision of the shape of things had been wrong. He had been afraid of Georges. In fact Georges had been afraid of him.

But Derek and Pierre could not know that. As far as they were concerned Georges was a threat. He had been in the village that night. What had he seen? Had he seen them beating Petit Louis to death? And if he had, was he playing his own game? Was he going to blackmail them, too?

Mimosa. That had given Neville the clue. That was the place from which Derek had wanted to dump Petit Louis into the river. That's where Georges' body had been dumped.

And once Neville knew that, he knew he was in deep trouble.

'Neville's always had one reaction to trouble,' Mary told Alex. 'He runs and hides. As a child he used to run away and hide from his father. And on the night you and Simon were hunted along the river bed he had seen Derek and Pierre come in the gate and had left the house.'

Max said, 'Until then he had hidden himself away in his own body. He made himself "unavailable", so to speak. But he could walk all the time, and speak as well.

'He was frightened. He withdrew. We all thought it was because of being trapped in the rockfall. In fact it was what had happened just before that.'

No one mentioned the irony, not in Mary's presence anyway. Neville had maintained a state of speechlessness because it would stop him answering questions. Now he would never speak again. Derek's bullet had smashed his larynx.

Alex shivered. The sun had gone down into the sea and the wind was cool. Yet she was not only cold because the day was dying. There was a secondary chill – of the spirit.

She rose to fetch a cardigan and as she did so she saw David and Simon coming up the path from the beach: the tall, loose-limbed man with the dark, untidy hair, and the young boy, still raw from his mother's death but masking it beneath a carapace of arrogance. The protective shell had helped in the recent events. He was quiet and subdued for some days but now he was beginning to recover.

As she watched them she felt again a sense of not belonging. She had experienced something similar in David's house in London. And she desperately wanted to belong to someone, to have the security of someone else's love. Not partially as she did now, but completely. She felt that very strongly. It had come out of the events in Carriac. She heard David and Simon arguing as they came to the house. They were always arguing about something. This morning it had been about the temperature of the Atlantic Ocean near the Azores, as if either could have known for certain.

At first she had worried about these arguments. Then she had worried when Simon became subdued and didn't argue. Now she realised that this was how they naturally reacted to each other. She had also discovered that Simon patronised his father just as much as he patronised her, which was a relief.

'Hi!' she called down.

'Hi yourself!' David called in reply.

She heard them clattering up the stairs and in a moment they were out on the balcony.

David was holding a shell in his hands. 'What's this called?' he said. 'I say it's a clam. Simon says it's a "trough" shell – whatever that is.'

'Well, it is!' Simon said.

Alex knew what it was. She could see her father picking one up on the beach near their home in Sussex. He had known about shells.

'It's an oval venus,' she said, and her tone indicated certainty.

Simon scowled at her, then his eyes dropped. 'Is it really?' he said.

'Yes, darling, really. We used to find them at West Wittering.'

'When we get back home,' he said directly to her, 'can we go and look for shells?'

'Of course. And we needn't take your father.'

'No, he doesn't know anything about them.'

'My God,' David said, wryly, 'if this is what it's going to be like I need a drink.'

'Me too,' she said. 'I've finished the article.'

He went in to get the wine and Simon went about his affairs.

She was alone, yet not alone. Remember this, she thought. Remember this moment.